This novel is dedicated to my wife, Sue, and my two sons, James and William, with much love. Thank you so much for all our holidays in the South of France. Hopefully, one day, it will be our home.

Acknowledgments

I would like to thank my wife, Sue, for her patience, support and advice as I was writing this novel. I love you so much and you're still my best friend!

My thanks, too, for all the advice and constructive criticism I received from my dear friends, Daphne Griffiths, Moira Walker and my sister-in-law, Suzanne John (who is as sarcastic and as good a critic as my wife).

Moira Walker and her husband, Bill, are very good friends. Moira was formally a senior infection control nurse in Vancouver General Hospital; she now lectures on the subject across Canada. Her knowledge of hospital procedures and drugs were invaluable in the writing of this novel. I can't thank her enough for her help.

In the early stages of this book, before it had the whiff of a publisher or agent, I relied heavily on my two main informal editors, who are also my most critical readers. So to my wife (Sue) and sister-in-law (Suzanne), I offer my sincerest thanks.

I would also like to acknowledge all our friends in Provence, who helped me with the research – and Alan Collier and his wife, in the Dordogne, who advised me on the French sections of the text.

Finally, I must give special recognition to a wild, mad storm one day in Var, which inspired me to create *The Milk of Paradise*.

THE MILK OF PARADISE

THE MILK OF PARADISE

Nigel Gallimore

ATHENA PRESS
LONDON

ISBN 1 84401 807 5

First Published 2006 by
ATHENA PRESS
Queen's House, 2 Holly Road
Twickenham TW1 4EG
United Kingdom

Printed for Athena Press

Author's Note

Although all the towns and locations described in this novel exist, the hotel La Maison does not. I've no idea if there really is a tunnel linking Bargemon with Callas but there are plenty of such constructions scattered all over Provence. The priest escape tunnel that surrounds the nearby village of Seillans gave me the inspiration for the escape route at La Maison.

Storms, such as the one described in *The Milk of Paradise*, are quite regular during the summer in Var. They rarely inflict such devastating damage; but one that Sue and I encountered driving on a mountain road outside Callas during the summer of 1985 as we were visiting friends in Bargemon did cause a great deal of disruption. It was also very frightening and gave me the idea for the storm in this novel.

Provence, Var especially, is like a second home to us and this novel is for all the wonderful, hospitable Provençals who have become our friends over the years.

Remember, though, whilst all the locations (except La Maison) exist, this is just a story and all the events, situations and characters in this novel are fictitious. Any resemblance to any situation or persons either living or dead is purely coincidental. It was all conjured up in my mind and from my love of Provence.

And all should cry, Beware! Beware!
His flashing eyes, his floating hair!
Weave a circle round him thrice,
And close your eyes with holy dread!
For he on honey-dew hath fed,
And drunk the milk of Paradise.

S T Coleridge
Xanadu

Provence, August 2005

One

Five kilometres from the Provençal village of Bargemon, shrouded by aromatic pine trees and positioned away from its isolated mountain access road, stands La Maison, an exclusive hotel in the South of France. Scattered around the grounds are numerous fragrant bushes of rosemary, lavender and thyme – the perfume of Provence. Place a foot anywhere amongst the coarse Mediterranean grass and a profusion of blue, red and brown winged cicadas leap aside, revealing the source of the deafening chirruping. Butterflies and moths flutter around, absorbing the dry, hot heat of the day in an almost infinite diversity and number. The whole area buzzes with such a multitude of wildlife that it seems impossible to imagine that this is anything other than paradise.

It was in this idyllic setting that Georges and Maria Ribert ran their profitable holiday business, which catered exclusively for British tourists. Couples and families from all over the United Kingdom arrived during Saturday afternoons, at fortnightly intervals throughout the spring and summer to experience and indulge in the very essence of Provençal hospitality.

It was late afternoon on a Saturday during mid-August that Georges and Maria Ribert were awaiting the arrival of their eight guests. They had bought the house a decade ago from the local Catholic church. It had been abandoned and left to ruin when the priest moved to a property closer to the town.

The Riberts had thoroughly researched the needs and desires of their clientele. As a result, they had built up a very successful tourist operation and had secured a multitude of loyal, regular guests who returned year after year to this paradise in the sun. Georges was the chef at La Maison and, like so many great French cooks, had acquired his skills and passion for food from his parents. He used fresh, local ingredients and lavished loving care on everything he prepared. Living in the region of Var – the heart of Provence – he had access to the very best produce; but it was the attention he gave to every facet of cooking that was responsible for his success and reputation. He meticulously planned all the menus, his experience acting as a guide to how he would create and develop each meal. Georges was a very contented man. He was successful, loved his job and planned to take on more staff.

There was, however, a dark side behind the idyllic façade of Georges and Maria Riberts' successful business venture. It was indiscernible to the local population and the innocent visitors who flocked annually to this outwardly benign tourist area of Var. In reality, there was an undercurrent of deceit and deception that, if mishandled, could conceivably rock the very foundations of French and Western society. This was an area notorious amongst international intelligence agencies as being the doorway to Europe for drugs traffickers, arms traders and terrorists throughout the world. It was virtually impossible to adequately police the numerous secluded sections of the rugged coastline and the Riberts had taken full advantage of their isolated location to use La Maison as a major distribution point for illegal merchandise.

The afternoon began to slip by as Georges was in the kitchen making the final preparations for the evening meal. Suddenly, there was an announcement on the radio that made him stop his work and listen intently. He carefully took note of the content of the broadcast and looked out towards the terrace where his wife was lying by the side of the swimming pool, soaking up the hot afternoon sun. The baking heat radiated over her whole body as she shared the terrace with insects and lizards on this peaceful Provençal afternoon. Their daughter, Monique, was swimming strongly in the warm iridescent water. As Maria watched her daughter, she dangled a hand into the pool and splashed gently with her fingers, causing the bright sun to shine through the droplets of water, dispersing the light into flickering colours of the spectrum. She lay back, relaxing in the warmth of the afternoon, and reflected once again on her good fortune. The tranquillity was interrupted by Georges who unexpectedly appeared on the patio looking concerned.

'What's wrong?' asked his wife.

'I was listening to the radio in the kitchen. They've just put out a storm warning in our area for tomorrow night. They're suggesting it could be the worst we've had here for over a hundred years and say we must expect a lot of structural damage.'

'Oh no! That's just what we need at the height of the tourist season.'

Monique swam over to the edge of the pool to be by her parents so that she could clearly hear everything her father was saying.

'They said there is likely to be some isolated flash flooding and are warning people not to go out unless it is absolutely necessary.'

'We'll be alright up here in the mountains though, won't we?' asked Maria.

'I should think so, but we'll have to warn the guests.'

'I don't think we should spoil their first night in Provence,' answered Maria. 'There's not going to be a problem this evening, is there?'

'No. The forecast for tonight is good.'

'That settles it, then. We won't mention it to them until to-morrow morning.'

'Won't they have heard about it on their car radios?' asked Monique. 'Wouldn't it be better to tell them straight away?'

Maria looked at her husband and they both laughed.

'Have you forgotten that they are British tourists?' asked her mother cynically. 'Do you really think any of them will be able to speak much French?'

Monique smiled and pulled herself out of the water.

'Mama, I'm going to pop down to the town for the rest of the afternoon to have a drink with some friends. You don't need me here until it's time to serve dinner, do you?'

'That's fine. Go and enjoy the rest of the afternoon.'

They watched her go. It was still hard for them to accept that their eighteen-year-old daughter was no longer their little girl.

She had grown up so quickly and now she was destined to leave them and move into an apartment with her boyfriend from the village. Georges sighed as he watched his daughter depart and turned back to his wife, whom he sensed was becoming increasingly anxious with their precarious situation. He waited until he was quite sure Monique was out of earshot before saying, 'Are you more relaxed now about the next few days?'

'Not really. Also, Georges, you do realise that most of the people coming today will be able to speak French quite well!'

'I know, *mon chéri*, but we must maintain the pretence. Monique mustn't suspect anything is wrong.'

'We shouldn't have agreed to do this!'

'There wasn't any choice. You know that!'

'Maybe, but I still think it was irresponsible to let that newly-married couple book in at the last minute. We should have told them that we were full.'

'No, Foxicat is beginning to get suspicious. They've already tapped our phone lines and we know they have the resources to intercept our post. They would have been fully aware that we had a room free and if we had tried to put off those last minute guests it might have looked suspicious.'

'How did we get involved with all this? I'm so scared.'

'I am too, but they have always paid us well and if it wasn't for Foxicat we wouldn't have this hotel.'

'We didn't have to become double agents, did we? If Foxicat ever finds out that we've been informing the intelligence agencies about CAT activities he'll have us killed!'

Georges looked at her with mounting concern; he knew only too well the heartless sadists that Foxicat employed as assassins.

'If we hadn't agreed to cooperate with the government's investigators, we would have been imprisoned for drugs trafficking. If you remember, they threatened to lock us away for a minimum of twenty years unless we helped them with this particular case.'

'Georges, you are fully aware, I hope, that I've never been comfortable dealing in drugs?'

'You still took the money quite happily!'

Maria ignored the comment. 'What we've been asked to do this time is completely different.'

'Is it?'

'Yes, it is, and I don't understand how you can't see that. If those biological weapons get through, then we'll be responsible for genocide on an unimaginable scale. We shouldn't be doing this!'

'That's precisely why they're sending the special agents. It's their job to ensure the consignment doesn't get through to London.'

'CAT has contacts everywhere; you know that! I'm very worried about the consequences if they discover that we colluded with the authorities.'

'That isn't going to happen. As far as the outside world is concerned, we have a hotel full of paying guests, as is usual for this time of the year. They will pretend to be tourists, whilst carrying out their investigation discreetly. All we have to do is pass the consignment down the line, just as we've always done. The agents will do the rest and no one will suspect us of anything.'

'I'll tell you what, Georges, these agents had better be as good as they are hyped up to be or we'll be in deep shit!'

'The delegate who contacted me from Lyon was adamant that they're all experienced, top-class British secret service officers!'

Maria looked at him sharply before continuing. 'I suppose you've realised that if they do break this smuggling chain we'll have lost a significant part of our income?'

'We'll still have the hotel business and hopefully one day CAT will reopen our line. After all, there aren't many places around here as well designed for storing and moving around illegal merchandise.'

'I'll still be glad when all of this is over. I just don't like having to put on an act all the time, always pretending we're just leading a normal life. And I'm not happy about lying to CAT!'

'We've been living double lives ever since we became caught up with these terrorists and we have to maintain the illusion! You know that I suspect CAT has us under surveillance. Our only hope is that the intelligence services are able to infiltrate this terrorist cell without our role in it being uncovered.'

'We could do without this storm, too. The last thing we want is for the shipment to be delayed.'

'Let's not even think about that—' began Georges, but he was interrupted by the sound of a car entering the grounds. He glanced in the direction of the approaching vehicle.

'Our first guests are arriving, so let's do what we do best and make them feel welcome.'

Maria looked at her husband apprehensively, leapt up and dashed into the house in order to greet the first set of visitors.

A black Peugeot 206 pulled up in one of the parking bays. There were faint red markings on the rear side windows and body work of the car, remnants of graffiti scrawled by friends at the couple's wedding reception in Essex. Ben and Carla O'Sullivan had booked into La Maison for their honeymoon. Ben, a chemistry teacher in Greater London, was tall, well proportioned and athletic. He had a small, straight nose, which was perfectly balanced by his attractive, angular face. A suggestion of dark stubble, the result of travelling overnight, complemented his light brown eyes and black, wavy hair. Ben jumped out of the car, flexed his muscles and sighed contentedly as he stretched and looked up at the hotel building. He glanced over to his wife as she disentangled herself from the maps and debris at her feet.

Carla O'Sullivan had light brown hair that fell straight to her shoulders, accentuating her pale complexion and light blue eyes. Once out of the car, she too looked up expectantly at the building and thought that it was exactly as she had imagined it to be from the description on the hotel website. A colleague at work had told Ben about a peaceful hotel in the South of France that offered a fortnight full board. At the earliest opportunity he looked it up on the Internet and made contact via email. They had both been excited to discover that there was a vacancy that fitted in perfectly with their wedding plans. He made a reservation, and from what he had discerned from the booking conditions, there were no other arrangements that needed to be made – other than to pay for additional drinks.

Ben seized two suitcases from the boot and they both made their way to the hotel entrance. The dark and pleasantly cool reception area contrasted starkly with the brightness of the hot, dazzling sun. It took a few moments for their eyes to become accustomed to the drastic change in light, but once focused Ben and Carla went straight to the reception desk and rang the bell.

The quietness of the hall was broken as the jarring peal echoed around the interior of the building, startling them both. A few moments later, Maria Ribert entered, smiling welcomingly.

'*Bonjour*,' stammered Ben clumsily. '*Monsieur et Madame O'Sullivan. Nous avon reservations.*'

Ben looked quite relieved to have passed the test of speaking a foreign language and at the same time felt quite pleased with his effort.

'Welcome to La Maison,' Maria replied in perfect English.

Carla laughed. She had observed Ben become increasingly agitated as they made their final approach to the hotel. She knew that he was nervous about speaking a foreign language. His anxiety had been heightened by his brother, Scott, who was fluent in several languages and had been teasing Ben remorselessly as he rehearsed his introductory speech before leaving for France.

'If it's alright with you, we usually find it best to speak in English,' continued Maria. 'Then there can be no confusion about any of the arrangements.'

'English will be fine,' said Ben, feeling very relieved and much more relaxed. 'I'm afraid my French isn't very good, but your English is excellent.'

'Thank you. I taught myself before we opened the hotel.'

'You put us to shame,' added Carla. 'I'm afraid my French is even worse than my husband's.'

Maria smiled at her kindly, acknowledging Carla's admission of inadequacy.

'I'm sure that you must be very tired after your journey,' said Maria. 'Let me show you to your room and you can freshen up.'

They followed her up the stairs to their room. Wooden shutters across the windows and a heavy curtain over the door of their private balcony offered good protection from the hot sun. After Maria Ribert had left, Carla went out onto the terrace and gazed at the spectacular views across the rough, awesome mountain terrain. She had been told about the bright light and colours of Provence being different from anywhere else and now she was witnessing this for herself. Nothing she had read had been exaggerated. The magical enchantment of southern France had seduced her. She turned to her husband.

'I think I've fallen in love with Provence already, Ben! I'm so glad that we were persuaded to come here.'

Ben looked over at his wife and thought she was the most beautiful person he had ever met.

'Come over here,' he instructed.

She smiled and joined her husband, allowing him to embrace her.

As Ben and Carla immersed themselves in an afternoon of lovemaking, the next set of guests had almost reached the nearby town of Bargemon. The approach to the town was both impressive and daunting. The road was narrow and wound steeply around the mountainside with unprotected drops into the valley below. As her husband navigated the narrow mountain road, Susan Chapman stared out of the window, admiring the specially-adapted, water-conserving xerophytic plants that clung desperately to the hot surface of the rock. She thought they added a welcome colour to the inhospitable barren environment, as they cascaded strikingly over the side of the limestone escarpment.

Her husband glanced up into his rear-view mirror and observed a small van dash up to them at an alarming speed.

'Here's another loon! I suppose they think by sitting on the tail-end of my bumper it will intimidate me into driving faster?'

Susan glanced behind her nervously.

'Don't you dare go any faster, Michael!'

'Don't worry, I've held out so far.'

'Make sure that you continue to resist it! I don't particularly relish the thought of being road-raged by one of these hot-headed French drivers.'

They reached a small, straight section of road and the van dashed past them recklessly, whilst the driver blasted his horn.

'I wish they wouldn't do that,' said Susan. 'It's so unnecessary.'

Michael was totally unmoved by the histrionics and continued to drive attentively. Susan quickly recovered from her fright and continued to gaze at the scenery, jumping less at the blaring horns as she gradually became habituated to the local traffic. They eventually turned a corner and saw the medieval town of

Bargemon perched perilously on the side of the mountain. They entered the village by a narrow road that was lined with ancient plane trees.

The centre of the village was at a junction marked by a small fountain that Susan noted seemed to act as an unofficial round-about for the local population. To the right of the fountain was a bar and restaurant where locals and tourists alike sat in the shade of the trees, sipping pastis and beer. Michael steered the car anti-clockwise around the fountain and onto the road that would take them to their destination of La Maison.

A few minutes later, they parked by the side of Ben and Carla's car, relieved their journey was at an end. As Susan reached into the boot to pick up a suitcase, a church bell rang out four times. She looked at her watch and noted it was two minutes past four. She was just about to comment on the time when another bell pealed four times. The second bell had a much duller pitch than the first and this one was three minutes late.

'That's interesting,' said Susan. 'Have you noticed that those bells are not only unsynchronised, but are both incorrect?'

'Well that's Provence for you. They don't seem to bother much with conventions around here, or the law, which is, of course, why we're here!'

Susan glanced over somewhat nervously to her husband as a blue BMW screeched into the drive. Michael saw it and addressed his wife: 'Here we go, and don't forget we have never met any of these people before.'

'I know, Michael. I'm not a fool!'

The car skidded to a halt by their side. A tall, slender woman stepped out of the car. She was in her early thirties with long, straight brown hair and dazzling, dark green eyes.

'Hello,' she said to Michael. 'My name is Andrea Baker, and this is my husband, James.'

James Baker was tall and blond and his open, short sleeved shirt revealed a slim, hairless, sun-bronzed body. They shook hands and Michael introduced himself and his wife to the new arrivals. They all assumed their roles perfectly.

'Did you have a good journey?' asked Michael politely.

'Not too bad,' answered Andrea. 'The autoroute was very busy and quite slow in places, but my goodness, the drivers around here are all completely bonkers, aren't they?'

'They are indeed,' said Michael. 'I suppose we'll soon get used to these mountain roads. Although, I really can't see me ever overtaking a vehicle on a blind bend as everyone seems to do here!'

By seven o'clock that evening they were all on the terrace close to the dining area, which was set amongst olive trees. Colin and Sarah Radley had also arrived for their two-week break in the sun during the late afternoon. The Riberts had soon discovered that guests at La Maison always preferred to eat outside on the terrace in the warm evening sun, rather than in the dining room. An interesting aroma diffused through the olive grove from the kitchen, tempting their appetite, as they expectantly sipped their aperitifs. They sat looking out over the pool; the cicadas chirruped more loudly than ever and the air was full of a multitude of coloured insects.

'This is just fabulous!' said Ben. 'I don't think we could have chosen a better place to spend our honeymoon.'

'Your friend said the food is excellent too,' added Carla. 'I wonder what we are going to have tonight.'

'It looks like we are having some sort of salad,' said Ben as he observed Maria placing frosted glass bowls full of *salade niçoise* on their tables.

They all finished their aperitifs and took their places at tables on the terrace. The background sound of the wildlife dominated the evening air as the diners enthusiastically devoured their salad.

'Fabulous!' exclaimed Colin Radley as he stretched back and licked the final traces of the perfumed olive oil from his lips. 'If all the food is of this quality, we won't have any complaints over the next two weeks.'

'The fish in this salad is like nothing I have ever tasted before,' enthused his wife, Sarah. 'The sardines had a slight smokiness to them; he must have barbequed them and then flaked it with the tuna. I think it might be the nicest salad I have ever eaten!'

'I'm glad you enjoyed it so much,' said Maria, overhearing the compliments as she was clearing away the dishes. 'That salad is one of the specialities of Provence.'

'What have we got next?' asked Sarah.

All the guests turned around expectantly, eager to discover what was to follow. Carla was suddenly aware how striking Sarah was. She wasn't particularly beautiful, but the angular bone structure of her face, coupled with a natural elegance, made people notice her. Carla turned her attention back to Maria Ribert.

'It is one of my husband's specialities, *Torte de Lapereaux*. I think in English you would call it rabbit pie.'

'I've never eaten rabbit,' confessed Sarah. 'It will be an interesting first for me.'

The rabbit pie turned out to be another culinary masterpiece and caused a sensation amongst the diners.

'Well,' said Ben after he had ordered a second bottle of wine, 'it's a bit of a travesty calling that rabbit pie. Wasn't it wonderful?'

'Yes,' agreed Carla. 'I've never fancied rabbit before, but that was fantastic!'

'Well, being an Essex boy, I used to eat rabbit quite a lot when I was young. I used to go out shooting them during the harvest with my brother, Scott, but it never tasted as good as this pie, though.'

'I didn't know that you used to shoot!'

'Yes. Scott and I used to enter tournaments together.'

'Actually, I can imagine both you and Scott doing that,' she said. 'You two are both so competitive.'

'The little bugger always beat me on the shooting range,' he said grinning. 'He was an excellent shot, so it came as no surprise to us when he joined the army after finishing uni. Don't forget to remind me to text him later to let him know that we arrived here safely.'

Carla looked at her husband tenderly. When Carla had first started to date Ben, she had occasionally found herself feeling slightly jealous of his close relationship with Scott. But over the years she had grown to love Scott dearly – especially for his loyalty to Ben.

After they had finished their meal, the guests went to sit out by the swimming pool. It was beginning to get dark and the cicadas seemed more active than normal. As darkness descended, they all noticed the beauty of the night sky. It glistened and twinkled with thousands of bright pinpricks of light, all set in the clear blackness of the universe.

As the others stared upwards, mesmerised by the night sky, James and Colin wandered off into the grounds alone to spot wild boar. Ben and Carla were so absorbed in each other, they didn't even notice them leave.

When they were away from the house, Colin began the conversation.

'We will have to be careful, in case this place is under surveillance,' said Colin urgently. 'I received a warning just before I left that CAT are onto us.'

'How could they possibly know anything?' asked James, shocked.

'We know the French police have been infiltrated, so it's possible our own organisation has been, too.'

'What about the owners of this hotel; could they be double-crossing us?'

'No, we've frightened them enough into assisting us,' answered Colin. 'They are quite aware that, if we suspect them of anything, they'll be in prison for the next thirty years. They wouldn't dare let us down. Anyway, all we'd have to do is to leak a report to Foxicat informing him that they have been helping us and they'd be dead meat – and they know it!'

'Are we going ahead as planned tomorrow?'

'Yes. I'll take Sarah to Les Baux on a sightseeing excursion and you go to the beach with Andrea.'

'What about Michael?'

'I'll drop a note under his door tonight to give him further instructions.'

They returned quickly to the terrace to find the others still gazing up at the stars.

'I don't think I have ever seen a sky like this,' they heard Carla say to her husband.

'No,' said Ben staring intently at the sky. 'I suppose it is because we live in such a polluted environment as London, which explains why our night sky doesn't ever look like that.'

'It's beautiful,' whispered Carla.

'Look!' exclaimed Andrea suddenly, attracting everyone's attention.

They all glanced up, following her gaze. She was staring in the direction of a large tree by the side of the house. Around it were several flickering and moving spots of light, like specks of silvery glitter falling through a moon beam. They watched, captivated, for several minutes as the fireflies continued their courtship dance against the back drop of the dense black sky. They were interrupted by Monique Ribert bringing them their latest drinks orders.

'You live in a fabulous place,' said Ben to Monique, as she passed him a glass of wine.

'Yes, we do,' she agreed. 'It really is lovely sitting out at night and watching the stars.'

'It's such a warm evening that I feel like sitting out here all night watching the heavens,' replied Ben.

Monique laughed. 'I often do that myself.'

They were interrupted by James Baker, who got up and came over to them.

'I heard on the local radio, whilst we were driving to the hotel, that there might be a bad storm here tomorrow night,' he said. 'So, we might not be able to sit out very late tomorrow.'

He turned to Monique, as the others all looked over in dismay. 'Have you heard anything about it?'

Everyone turned round to listen.

'There is a storm warning for tomorrow night and it could be quite a violent one. My mother didn't want to spoil your first evening, so she wasn't going to tell you about it until the morning.' She turned to James. '*Parlez-vous Français?*'

'*Oui, il y a des Anglais qui parlent Français!*'

Monique laughed and replied in French. 'I'm sure there are some English people who speak my language. I just don't come across them very often!'

Colin looked over to him angrily but James was too involved in his banter with Monique to notice the non-verbal rebuke.

'Oh no,' said Ben, interrupting their conversation. 'We've come to the Mediterranean to get away from such weather. Please don't say it's going to change!'

'Don't worry about it,' laughed Monique, immediately reverting to speaking English. 'The forecast is still for very hot weather, but we do sometimes get late-night storms during August. It's nothing to worry about except that they can be quite violent and this one, apparently, is going to be fairly bad.'

'The worst for over a hundred years, according to the announcer on the radio this afternoon,' added James unnecessarily.

The others looked over to Monique, slightly alarmed.

'Please don't worry about it,' she reassured them. 'We're quite high up in the mountains so there isn't any risk of flooding. The worst thing that can happen is that we have a power failure for a couple of hours.'

'What a bummer,' said Ben, relaxing slightly. 'I hope it'll only be for one night.'

'It should be,' reassured Monique. 'We had intended to warn you about it tomorrow morning, because a storm in this region can be quite frightening if you haven't experienced one before.'

The sun was shining brightly the next day as Colin and Sarah Radley drove to the ancient hill top town of Les Baux de Provence. On arrival, they made their way to the fourteenth-century house, Musée Lapidaire, which acted as the ticket office and entry point to the ruined upper town. As they entered the area, the blistering heat hit them since they no longer had protected shade from buildings. The sound of the hot wind whistling around the ruins was almost deafening. They had read about the persistent, strong hot winds that raged continually around the unprotected section of the upper town and so they were not unprepared for the assault on their senses.

'It's incredible how this wind is suddenly all around you,' shouted Colin to his wife as they negotiated the barren plateau. 'You have no indication of it, even a few metres away in the lower town.'

'This is exactly how the guidebooks describe it,' answered Sarah. 'It really is quite amazing.'

'The wind feels so hot too,' continued Colin. 'You wouldn't be able to stay out in it for very long.'

'Apparently the air becomes superheated due to a combination of the hot sun and reflected heat from the white rock. I was reading that even the Mistral can feel hot when it sweeps across this plateau in the summer.'

'Why can't you feel the wind further down the valley?' asked Colin, suddenly developing an interest in the area's topography.

'It's something to do with the individuality of this single plateau,' explained Sarah, who had made a comprehensive study of the area before leaving home. 'It creates an air current that continually swirls the air around this upper section. It's completely unique to this specific area.'

'You're beginning to sound more like a guidebook,' said Colin, slightly sarcastically. 'Maybe your next job should be working as a tourist rep!'

Sarah laughed.

'Maybe it should! At least if I worked here I'd manage to get a permanent tan!'

Colin laughed too and they continued with their exploration.

On the side of the small ruined chapel was a large, bare limestone plateau. It was sparsely distributed with rough grass and herbs, which only just managed to survive the harsh environment. The perimeter of the plateau was a vertical drop to the foothills below and was completely unsecured. Colin and Sarah made their way towards the ruined upper town, which ran parallel with the rocky plateau. The wind had worked hard over the centuries to make impressive carvings into the tormented rocks. They took shelter from the hot sun in an eroded alcove.

'I'll tell you what,' said Colin, after he finally caught his breath. 'They really could do with a bar selling cool beer and water!'

'You can say that again! Even though there's a strong wind, it's still very hot.'

'Shall we try to climb up to the top of the citadel? Then maybe we could have a quick look over the Camargue from the plateau before going back to the lower town for a drink?'

To gain access to the citadel they had to navigate some very steep, uneven narrow stone steps. The constant trampling of feet over the centuries, along with the unrelenting strong winds, had eroded the path heavily. They carefully negotiated their way along, holding on tightly to the precarious rope railings. At the top, the wind whistled ruthlessly in their ears. They could hardly hear each other speak. The scenery, however, made the discomfort of the wind and heat all worthwhile. The panoramic view was breathtaking. It was a cloudless day and they could clearly see across the Rhone valley into the marshes of the Camargue, which was several kilometres away. The white limestone rock reflected the sun's rays directly onto their unprotected bodies, making the heat blisteringly uncomfortable. Colin looked down at the entrance point to the upper town and exclaimed loudly as he recognised two of the tourists.

'Look Sarah! Isn't that Ben and Carla from the hotel down there?'

Sarah looked down in the direction of Colin's stare and saw Ben and Carla entering the upper section of the ruin.

'Yes, it is. That's a bit of a coincidence isn't it? They didn't mention that they were coming here.'

He thought no more of it and continued to admire the spectacular scenery. Sarah, however, glanced furtively in Ben and Carla's direction.

'Come on,' said Colin, not noticing his wife's agitation. 'Let's go and have a look over at the other side of the plateau.'

'I'm not looking forward to negotiating those steep steps,' confessed Sarah. 'I'm beginning to wish that I had stayed down below.'

'You'll be fine. Just hold on tightly to the rope.'

They cautiously descended the precarious, misshapen steep steps, hardly daring to look down. After what seemed an eternity, they reached the bottom and were both relieved to have their feet on firm ground again. They made their way slowly from the ruined citadel and onto the barren exposed plateau. The wind was almost unbearable as it howled mercilessly in their ears. A golden eagle was circling around the valley, keenly watching for prey. They glanced up and watched it for a few minutes before continuing their journey towards the precipice.

'I can't see that this is very safe,' said Sarah, stopping a couple of metres from the cliff edge. 'There should be safety barriers here. You could easily tumble over the cliff face.'

'What was that?' shouted Colin as he continued to move towards the edge, the wind carrying the sound of his wife's cautious words away from him.

On the opposite cliff face, Carla caught sight of Colin and Sarah. She turned back to look at the views and was about to tell Ben about seeing two of the other guests from the hotel when she heard screaming. They both turned sharply and saw Sarah standing by the cliff face screaming wildly. They ran over to Sarah and grabbed hold of her.

'What's the matter?' demanded Carla.

'Oh my God, it's Colin!' screamed Sarah hysterically.

Sarah looked up at Carla, shaking uncontrollably and incapable of replying. Carla looked around, suddenly realising that Colin had disappeared from sight. She turned her attention back to Sarah, who she could see was unable to speak. Carla assumed this was because she was disorientated as a result of what ever had happened on the dusty plateau. She took a pack of tissues from her pocket and passed one over to Sarah, instructing her to wipe away the tears and mucus gushing freely from her eyes and nose. Carla turned to Ben and for the first time noticed that they were surrounded by concerned-looking tourists. Sarah was still unable to speak, so Carla turned desperately to the gathering crowd.

'Is there any one here who speaks English?'

'Yes,' came back three voices.

'Did anyone see what happened?' she asked as Sarah continued to cry hysterically.

None of the English speakers had. One of them turned to the remaining crowd and asked in French if anyone else had seen what had happened. Again, no one had – all they had heard were Sarah's screams.

Ben grabbed hold of Sarah firmly. 'Sarah, what happened?'

She looked up slowly into Ben's eyes, her vacant expression convincing him that her bewilderment was genuine.

'It's Colin, he fell over the cliff!'

'Oh my God!' exclaimed Ben. 'How the hell did that happen?'

'I don't know,' replied Sarah, sounding more distant.

'What do you mean, "you don't know," Sarah?' asked Ben in disbelief. 'You must have seen it?'

She looked towards the cliff edge, but was unable to discern anything that made any sense. Everything around her was becoming blurred and confused. Internally, she was wracked with pain and despair. She bit into her trembling bottom lip, piercing the skin and experienced a sickening feeling, which confirmed this wasn't a dream. Her nose was still running as she eventually attempted a coherent explanation.

'He was just looking at a bird flying overhead, then I think a gust of wind must have caught him and knocked him off balance. I was telling him not to go too near the edge and he just—'

She wept hysterically again as Ben and Carla looked on in shocked helplessness. Ben turned to the crowd and asked if anyone knew the number for the emergency services. One of the bilingual tourists used their mobile phone to contact the police and fire department.

Once he was quite sure the police were on their way, Ben said to Carla, 'I think we should stay with Sarah when the police arrive. I daren't go near the edge of the cliff, but I'm sure he can't have survived the fall.'

'How could something like this happen?' asked Carla incredulously. 'And how could no one have seen it?'

'I don't know.'

He turned back to Sarah. She was cold and shaking, completely oblivious to what was going on around her.

'Sarah,' he said firmly. 'The police are on their way. When they arrive we'll come with you.'

She stared up at him, neither seeming to hear or comprehend his words. In the distance, they heard the sound of police sirens and a helicopter was now circling above them. The police arrived and took Sarah, with Ben and Carla, to a hospital in the nearby town of St Remy de Provence. Whilst Sarah was being escorted to the hospital, the police took statements from all the tourists who could possibly have witnessed the accident. No one had seen Colin fall but everyone confirmed the presence of the strong wind. The police concluded that Les Baux de Provence had accumulated another victim to add to its turbulent and violent history.

The shocked guests were told of the death of Colin Radley during the late afternoon as they returned to the hotel from their various excursions. Sarah hadn't wanted to stay overnight at the hospital and the police made arrangements with Ben and Carla to drive her back to La Maison. She had been heavily sedated and, on arrival, Ben carried her unconscious body from the back of his car to the bedroom. Once there, Maria Ribert put her straight to bed and they left her to sleep, assisted by the strong medication.

Two

Later in the evening, the remaining guests sat together solemnly on the terrace, sipping wine. They had eaten Georges's *soupe de poisson* with bread soaked in garlic mayonnaise, followed by grilled, marinated lamb, as enthusiastically as the circumstances deemed appropriate. They were all stunned by the tragedy and the air around them matched their mood. As the evening progressed, the atmosphere began to feel heavy and oppressive as Provence readied itself for the forecasted storm. Carla was staring out into the night, still confused and shocked by the events she had witnessed. James watched her vigilantly, waiting for an appropriate opportunity to inquire after Colin's accident.

Carla spoke softly to Ben. 'I just looked over to them for a few seconds and turned back to look at the view when Sarah suddenly started to scream uncontrollably.'

Ben attempted to console his wife by placing his arm around her shoulder.

'It's probably best not to think about it. It was such a terrible thing to happen and I really think that you should try and put it out of your mind.'

'I can't, Ben, and I still don't understand how such a terrible thing could have happened.'

'You saw the terrain. It was completely open and I don't recall seeing many safety railings. It would have been so easy to be caught by a sudden gust of wind and be blown over the cliff.'

He stopped for a few moments and shuddered as he considered his ill-spoken words before adding: 'Of course, that's exactly what did happen, wasn't it, and the poor bastard didn't stand a chance!'

Carla winced.

'Don't Ben! But you're right; we shouldn't keep talking about it!'

James, who gradually eased himself closer to them, intervened.

'I'm sorry to interrupt,' he said apologetically. 'I've never been to Les Baux, so I don't know what the terrain is like, but what actually happened?'

'I'm afraid we didn't see anything at all. I remember catching sight of Colin and Sarah on the other side of the plateau. I turned back to tell Ben and suddenly Sarah started screaming. We rushed over but there was no sign of Colin anywhere. She just managed to tell us that he had been caught by a gust of wind and had fallen over the cliff.'

'It seems that he'd been completely absorbed by watching an eagle flying overhead,' added Ben. 'In fact, most people were watching it, because it was huge and was circling the entire area. It was very windy, too, although I don't remember the wind gusting suddenly. It seemed to be all around us all the time.'

'I'm not sure I agree with you, Ben. As I turned back to you, I do seem to recall there was a gust of wind and that's when she started to scream.'

'Did you see him fall?' asked James urgently.

'No, I've already told you. No one did.'

'How could no one have seen it?' Andrea interrupted incredulously. 'There must have been hundreds of people there! Surely, somebody must have seen something?'

'Apparently they didn't,' replied Ben, impatiently. 'Carla and I went with Sarah to the hospital as soon as the police and paramedics arrived and we gave our statements there. I remember wishing my brother was with me – he's fluent in French – but I'm pretty sure that the police said no one had seen him fall.'

'I still find that very hard to believe,' insisted Andrea. 'How could you be standing next to someone and not be aware they had stumbled and fallen over the edge of a cliff?'

'You'd have to be there to appreciate it,' said Carla, desperately wishing that she hadn't pursued this line of conversation. 'The wind was deafening and the sun reflecting off the white rock was blinding.'

'Also, it was lunchtime and so most of the tourists were in restaurants, all of which are in the lower section of the town,' added Ben.

'I see,' said James, not sounding very convinced.

Suddenly, and he wasn't quite sure why, Ben was becoming irritated by James's attitude. He was about to reply when his phone bleeped. Ben looked at the display, read the incoming text and grinned.

'Who was that from?' asked Carla.

'It's Scott. I left a message on his mobile. He's been to Upton Park watching West Ham and has just picked up my voicemail.'

He looked at his wife apologetically.

'I had better ring him back.'

'Of course,' said Carla, sensing an escape route from the conversation. 'You call him and I'll organise some more wine.'

'That's an excellent idea.'

Ben moved away from the group in the hope of securing a stronger signal on his mobile. He pressed speed dial number three and was soon in conversation with his brother, explaining everything that had happened and assuring Scott that, although shocked, both he and Carla were fine.

'We've got a frigging storm coming up tonight as well,' said Ben to his brother. 'This isn't quite the start to our honeymoon that we had planned.'

'No,' laughed Scott. 'I've not heard anything about it over here. Do you want me to look on the Internet and keep you updated?'

'Thanks, that would be very helpful. I hope it's not too much trouble.'

'I haven't got anything else to do,' admitted Scott ruefully. 'I'm home on leave and all my mates are either away on holiday or on their fucking honeymoon!'

Ben laughed.

'I thought you had a date tonight.'

'She turned out to be a right slapper so I got rid of her, presto pronto!'

'Sorry, mate. How was the football?'

'Don't ask!'

Ben laughed again.

'So we lost again?'

'Yeah, bloody West Ham United. Why are we both so loyal to them?'

'Because they're the best and we're not glory hunters,' Ben dutifully reminded him.

'You didn't see how they played!'

'Maybe, but can you give me a full match report when I'm back in England, Scott? This call will be costing me a fortune. I really ought to be getting back to Carla now.'

'OK. I'll track that storm for you. Could you text me in the morning to let me know that you're both safe?'

'I don't think it's going to be that bad, Scott,' laughed Ben. 'We're in the South of France, not in some bloody outback! But I'll contact you in the morning anyway.'

'Thanks. Night, Ben.'

In England, the line went dead and Scott closed the flip on his mobile phone. He was suddenly feeling uneasy about the situation in France. He went to the fridge, took out a bottle of beer and then went straight to his computer to log on to the Web. He connected quickly to the army website that would give him the most accurate information on the weather patterns in the South of France. He highlighted the region of Var on the map, took a swig of beer and frowned as he saw the deep depression forming, which threatened to bring a violent storm to the area. He opened up his phone and typed a text message.

Back in Provence, Ben's mobile phone bleeped again.

'Who's that text from?' asked Carla as Ben retrieved the message.

'Scott,' said Ben only half-listening to his wife as he read the text from his brother.

'What has he got to say?'

Ben didn't answer and passed his phone to Carla.

I HAVE LOOKED ON WEB 4 U. U R IN 4 A FUCKER OF A STORM. KEEP DRY. S.

Carla looked startled.

'Don't worry,' he tried to reassure her. 'We'll be alright here.'

He typed a reply to his brother's message.

THANX. WILL TEXT U WHEN IT'S OVER. B.

He sent the text and turned back to his wife.

'Scott's only confirmed what we already knew,' he said, trying his best to be reassuring. 'There's nothing to worry about.'

'I hope not. Actually, I wish I hadn't read that text.'

'What's the matter?' asked James, alert to their concerns.

Ben explained that his brother was an officer in the armed forces and that he had just confirmed a violent storm was on its way.

Maria and Georges Ribert, who had just arrived to replenish the drinks, looked at each other nervously as Ben told the other guests about Scott's text message. Suddenly there was a low, distant rumble of thunder in the background. It wasn't particularly loud but it was unexpected enough to startle them. The Riberts glanced at each other again as the thunder rumbled on. They had spent much of the day securing shutters and doors and ensuring objects in the garden couldn't blow around; the Riberts were taking no risks with the security of their property. They hadn't wanted to unduly alarm their guests, but the radio and local television station had warned that the storm could severely disrupt services and cause some damage in isolated areas. The wind was gradually building up and Georges could hear a shutter banging in an outbuilding at the rear of the property. He replenished his guests' wine and he and Maria left to complete a final check on the hotel.

'It looks like my brother was right about the storm,' said Ben, as a sudden gust of wind whistled round him. 'I hope it's cleared up by the morning.'

'Maria told me that they can be quite violent, but apparently they're soon over,' said James.

'Let's hope she's right,' answered Ben.

They spent the rest of the evening sitting on the terrace, listening to the sound of distant thunder. The cicadas were noticeably quieter and the thunder continued into the night.

Eventually, they all retired to bed and Maria and Georges Ribert were able to lock up the house.

'What are we going to do about this situation?' asked Andrea, once she and James were alone in their room. 'Now that Colin's dead, you're in charge of the operation.'

James looked at her carefully.

'We'll continue to operate the surveillance procedure as planned,' he said eventually. 'When I'm sure everyone's asleep, I'm going to make contact with Michael. I think we should check out the priest tunnel that links this house with Bargemon and Callas.'

They were interrupted by a loud clap of thunder. Andrea jumped and looked over towards the window. 'If this storm is as ferocious as has been predicted, then I don't suppose any of us will get much sleep tonight.'

'No, I don't suppose we will.'

He went over to the window and looked out into the darkness. Andrea could see he was feeling anxious and came over to him, placing her hand gently on his shoulder. 'Don't worry, James. Everything will work out alright.'

He looked into her eyes. 'I'm not so sure and it's beginning to worry me that the manoeuvre isn't progressing as we intended.'

Andrea looked startled. 'What do you mean?'

'I've been feeling uneasy since hearing the news that Colin had been killed and I'm still not comfortable sharing the hotel with those two lovebirds on honeymoon. They shouldn't have been allowed to come. If CAT suspects anything, there could be serious trouble.'

'The Home Office was quite adamant that they shouldn't be put off. They couldn't risk alerting CAT.'

James raised his eyebrows. 'I personally believe they're already suspicious and I don't trust the Riberts. Do you?'

'No.'

'Andrea, can you honestly tell me that you're one hundred per cent certain about everyone's identity? If you remember, we didn't receive photographs of Ben and Carla O'Sullivan, even though we requested them.'

'Are you suggesting that someone could have been substituted?'

'It's a possibility.'

Andrea looked troubled as James asked: 'Don't you think it was a bit of a coincidence that Ben and Carla were at Les Baux at the same moment Colin was killed?'

'No, I don't. He was blown off the cliff by the wind. It was an accident and Ben and Carla weren't anywhere near him.'

'That's what they said.'

'James, don't let your imagination run riot! Their explanation tallies with the account Sarah gave, so please get things into perspective. Colin was blown off a cliff by a sudden gust of wind and Carla and Ben had nothing to do with it.'

'Sarah's been unconscious since returning from Les Baux, hasn't she? We haven't heard an explanation from her. Again, we only have Ben and Carla's version and don't you think it's extraordinary that nobody witnessed it?'

'Carla said that everyone was looking at the views, so why do you consider it strange that no one saw the accident? The French police don't think it's suspicious.'

'We don't know that, do we? We haven't seen their report yet.'

'James, stop it. You're frightening me!'

'I didn't mean to. Sorry.'

'Perhaps we should drive over to St Remy in the morning and speak to the police officer in charge. If we show them an ID, they'll probably let us read their report.'

'That's a very good idea. Let's hope this bloody storm doesn't disrupt transport too much tomorrow.'

Andrea was about to comment further when she suddenly stopped as she observed a flicker of movement under the door of their room. She indicated for James to be quiet and moved swiftly and silently towards the door and quickly pulled it open. She jumped back, astounded to find Sarah Radley standing in their doorway.

'Sarah!' she exclaimed. 'What on earth are you doing?'

For a moment, Sarah didn't answer. Her eyes were glazed over and she appeared to be experiencing considerable difficulty in standing up straight. She swayed and Andrea quickly caught hold of her, skilfully supporting the sudden dead weight in her arms. When she had steadied, Sarah looked up at Andrea, obviously very dazed and confused.

'I'm sorry if I made you jump,' she said, with a slight slur. 'I've been wandering around aimlessly for a few minutes. I just can't seem to focus on anything.'

'That's alright,' said Andrea relaxing. 'You're still in a state of shock. Come on, I'll take you back to your room. Then maybe you should take some more of the sleeping tablets the hospital gave you.'

'No, I don't want to do that. They've made me feel terrible and my head's all fuzzy.'

'They may make you feel bad, but I still think you should take some and then lie down. You've had a terrible shock this afternoon and need to rest.'

James came over, looked suspiciously at Sarah and suggested: 'Perhaps when you've taken Sarah back to her room, you could talk to her about what happened.'

Andrea looked at him crossly.

'You can see she's not in any fit state to be questioned! There'll be plenty of time for that tomorrow morning,' she retorted and then turned her attention back to the semi-conscious woman. 'Come on, Sarah. Let me take you back to your bed.'

Sarah allowed herself to be escorted back to her room. Once there, she lay down and promised to try to get some sleep. As Andrea left the room, her mind was frantically trying to make sense of what James had been saying. She was now feeling very anxious about their situation, but common sense kept telling her that there wasn't any logic behind her misgivings. It was absurd to think that Colin's death was anything other than a dreadful accident, but James had made her feel uncomfortable. Was there a sinister menace surrounding the tranquil setting of La Maison, or had the recent events upset James to an extreme?

Logically, she shouldn't be at all threatened by their situation. Ben and Carla O'Sullivan were just tourists enjoying their honeymoon and there was no link between them and her mission in the South of France. It puzzled her why James had attempted to make an association, because there couldn't possibly be a connection between any of this and Colin's death. Nothing made any sense and yet Andrea was now beginning to feel increasingly concerned for all their safety.

As she left Sarah's room, there was a loud clap of thunder that coincided with a power failure. Andrea was plunged into darkness, a clammy, oppressive darkness like nothing she had experienced before. She couldn't see anything and this, along with the wind and thunder that raged around the house, compounded her terror. The pitch blackness disorientated her completely and she felt a panic attack welling up inside. Just as she was about to cry out and paw her way frantically forward, there was a bright beam of light in front of her. She instinctively followed it. Her heart was racing out of control and she was relieved to discover the welcome glow of light was from her husband's torch. She caught hold of him, taking comfort from his tight grip, and allowed him to lead her back to their bedroom.

'Typical of bloody France! The merest suggestion of a storm and all the lights go out!' he joked.

'I think this is more than the merest suggestion of a storm,' replied Andrea, relieved to be back in the safety of their room. 'Thank God you had a torch ready, James.'

'I suspected that we might have a power cut, so I made sure we had a torch accessible. By the way, what the hell was that woman doing outside our room?'

'I don't know, James. She was very confused and disorientated.'

'Did you ask her about the accident?'

'No. The medication the hospital gave her has completely wiped her out.'

'Oh well, maybe she'll be able to answer some questions in the morning. Now I think you should try to get some sleep. We have a lot to do tomorrow.'

Andrea agreed and snuggled up to James, jumping at each clap of thunder as the storm continued to deepen its grip.

Around two o'clock in the morning, the sky lit up in a terrifying blue incandescence, which was quickly followed by tremendously loud thunder. Then the rain started. The resonance of water droplets hitting the roof was deafening and it sounded like an onslaught of hard stones was crashing on the glass. In their rooms, the guests and owners of La Maison put their hands to their ears in an unsuccessful attempt to filter out the noise. Outside, telephone and electricity cables were ripped out, trees were felled and sections of the access road were washed away as the elements wreaked untethered havoc on the landscape. In the mountains, the rainfall developed into a massive torrent that swept down the valley, forming a terrifyingly spectacular wall of water. The artificial drainage channels proved to be totally ineffective as the force of the water and debris caused the built-in defence barriers to collapse. This had a shattering effect on the terrain, causing the water to grow in volume and force. It hurtled down the mountain, increasing in velocity and producing potentially devastating rapids. La Maison, along with the unprotected hillside towns of Bargemon and Callas were directly in its path.

Ben lay in bed with Carla clinging tightly to him. She was petrified by the developments outside and the roar of the water was becoming unbearable. Ben was suddenly aware of a dull background rumble, which was becoming increasingly audible over the loud shrapnel sound of the rain hammering on the roof. He sat up and listened to the sound in the distance.

'Whatever are you doing, Ben?'

'Listen. Can you hear that noise?'

'It's the rain hitting the roof. God, I wish it would stop!'

Ben was only half-listening to his wife as he prised his way out of Carla's grip and eased out of bed. He stood for a few moments listening to the storm. The dull resonance that he had first detected in the background was definitely increasing in volume. He struggled to keep calm.

'Carla, can you hear that low droning noise? It sounds a little bit like a light aircraft approaching.'

She listened for a few seconds before saying: 'Don't be ridiculous, Ben! An aircraft wouldn't be out in this weather.'

'Exactly!'

Using the limited light from the display on his mobile phone he made his way over to the shuttered terrace door.

'Carla, I'm going to try to open the shutters.'

'Don't be stupid, Ben!'

The sound seemed to be moving closer as Ben ignored his wife's pleas and opened the shutters. The rain was hitting the glass on their terrace door at an unbelievable speed and pressure, but Ben was undeterred.

'No, Ben!' Carla screamed against the thunderous clatter, suddenly realising what he was doing.

She jumped out of the bed and ran over to him, trying desperately to pull him away. Ben was so strongly driven by his desire to open the terrace door that he didn't even notice she was by his side. He continued to tug manically at the door, which had become caught up by the raging wind. It flew out of his hands smacking Carla sharply on the side of the head. The force of the impact flung her across the room and she smashed her head violently on the corner of the dresser. She lay on the floor motionless and Ben rushed over to her side. He grabbed hold of his wife, but her body was limp in his arms.

'Carla!' he shouted, but she gave no response. She had been knocked unconscious by the impact. Ben could see from the available dim light that she had a gaping lesion on the side of her head that was bleeding profusely. He laid her gently on the floor and used his phone to locate a torch. Once he had better light, he went to the bed and ripped off a section of the pillowcase to bind the wound. As he was tying it around her head, the bedroom door burst open and Michael and James rushed in, alerted by the screams and shouts. James flashed his torch around the room, immediately assessing the situation. He ran over to the terrace door and slammed it shut.

'What the fucking hell are you doing, you bloody idiot?' he demanded.

Ben wasn't listening, he was becoming increasingly transfixed by the low, dull rumble that had instigated his actions and that was noticeably increasing in volume. He stood up and began moving back to the external door.

'It doesn't matter what I'm doing!'

'What are you talking about?' shouted James. 'Why the hell did you open that door?'

Ben turned to him.

'If that sound in the background is what I think it is,' said Ben gravely, 'then we're all about to be either crushed to death or drowned. Listen!'

'I don't know what I'm supposed to be listening to! All I can hear is the rain!'

'Can't you hear that sound like a low-flying aircraft?' asked Ben. 'Except, I don't think it's an aircraft.'

James stopped and listened. He could hear it now. It was getting closer and increasing in volume. Andrea and Susan Chapman entered the room just as James was beginning to comprehend what was happening. They looked over at the three men who were going over to the terrace door looking extremely concerned. Then they too heard the sound.

'Whatever is that noise?' asked Andrea.

All eyes were suddenly on Ben.

'It's a torrent of water and it sounds as if it's heading straight for us!'

James forced the door open and along with Ben and Michael they battled their way onto the balcony. The wind and rain hit their faces with such ferocity that the pain was almost unbearable. They looked up into the darkness and could just make out a black cloud rolling towards them. At the last moment they realised it was a huge wall of water, which had formed as the massive volume of debris at the rear of the flood had surged forward, forcing the water ahead of it to rise upwards.

'Fuck!' whispered James.

Ben watched helplessly as the water descended on them.

'Well, at least Carla was spared this.'

The other two women were now at their side and began to scream. The water moved closer and Ben closed his eyes, accepting the inevitable. He had them closed for what seemed like an eternity. The reverberation of the moving water was unimaginable and almost burst his ear drums. Suddenly, he realised the moment had past. He opened his eyes to see James and his fellow victims staring upwards. Dense spray rained over them, but the building had remained intact.

'What's happening?' shouted Ben.

'It's washing over our heads and along the side of the house!' said James in disbelief. 'It hasn't hit us!'

They continued to watch with incredulous horror as the deluge of water passed them by. After a few seconds, it began to subside, the deafening roar slowly reducing in volume as the wind and rain began to settle down. Almost as rapidly as it had started, there was an abrupt and uncanny silence, which was interrupted by the sound of water dripping off surfaces. They all turned to look at each other in bewilderment.

'How could it have missed us?' asked Michael in amazement.

'I don't know,' answered James.

Ben suddenly snapped into the present and rushed over to his wife.

'Help me get her on to the bed,' he called out urgently.

They were joined by Maria and Georges Ribert who went over to Carla.

'What happened to her?' asked Georges.

'The door blew back and hit her across the room,' explained Ben. 'She smashed her head on the corner of this dresser. It knocked her unconscious.'

Georges bent down and gently put his face near hers.

'Will she be alright?' asked Ben desperately.

Georges looked up at him.

'She's breathing, but we need to get her to a hospital,' he answered quietly.

'I agree,' said James authoritatively. 'Ben, give Monsieur Ribert your mobile phone.'

Ben did as he was instructed and, as Georges Ribert contacted the emergency services, they moved Carla to the bed. James was suddenly aware that Sarah Radley and Monique Ribert weren't in the room.

'Where's your daughter?' he asked Georges.

Georges and Maria Ribert exchanged very worried glances.

'She's spending the night with her boyfriend, in Bargemon!'

The flow hit Bargemon just seconds after gushing past La Maison, enveloping homes, cars and trees instantly. The rock structure that had split the current in two, and spared La Maison from total destruction, had reduced the strength of the surge, causing the wall of water to drop back down. This had saved hundreds of lives in Bargemon, but it was still powerful enough to damage a significant section of the village.

In her boyfriend's flat, fortunately not in the path of the mud-slide, Monique clung desperately to her partner as the storm raged over the village. In the darkness she was completely unaware of the devastation to the section of the town that had been hit by debris. The roar was indescribable but, as at La Maison, it was over almost as quickly as it had begun. The peak of the storm diminished rapidly as it flowed down the valley so that, as it struck Callas, there was no more damage other than flooding of homes. The deep depression that had caused the storm had been confined to the immediate area surrounding Bargemon and the emergency services were activated at once.

La Maison had miraculously sustained very little damage. Just above the building was a rock formation that jutted upwards and out, almost overhanging the house. This caused the current to cascade over and around the sides of the house. The road leading down to the village of Bargemon had been washed away on both sides, isolating La Maison, without any power or telephone lines. Georges Ribert had been able to secure a weak signal on Ben's mobile phone and a helicopter arrived within fifteen minutes of making the call. The destruction to the surrounding terrain had made landing impossible, so the crew used their powerful searchlight beams to hover over the hotel and drop a line to lower a paramedic and stretcher into the grounds at the front of the house. Once on firm land, he rushed over to the building.

'*Ou est-elle?*' he demanded.

'*En haut,*' answered Georges. '*Suivez moi.*'

As instructed, the paramedic followed Georges up the stairs and into Ben and Carla's room. He went over to her, whilst Georges asked anxiously about the situation in Bargemon. '*Est-ce qu'il y a beaucoup des dégâts a Bargemon?*'

The paramedic looked up at him and confessed that he didn't know. '*Un coin de la vielle ville est enterré par la boue, mais la plupart reste intacte.*' Some of the old part of the town had been buried under a mud slide, but most of it was OK.

'Do you know anything about the newly-built block of flats by the school? My daughter's staying the night in one of them.'

'I think that part of the town is undamaged, but you must appreciate that we haven't been able to fully assess the situation yet.'

He turned his attention to Carla. Ben was by her side.

'Will she be alright?' Ben asked.

The paramedic looked at him blankly; he spoke no English. Georges had become preoccupied, frantically attempting to make contact with his daughter by mobile phone. His wife was clinging onto him and they had both ceased to concentrate on the situation with Carla. James took over and translated the exchange.

'He says that she will need to be taken to hospital in Draguignan. They're going to airlift her out now.'

'Will they let me go with her to the hospital? I can't let her go on her own.'

The paramedic looked up sharply at James and asked: '*Qu'est ce qu'il a dit?*'

'He says that he wants to go to the hospital with his wife,' James replied in French.

'*Non, ce n'est pas possible!*' he replied sharply. '*Il n'y a pas beaucoup de place dans l'hélicoptère et nous devons faire deux autres appels d'urgence avant revenir à l'hôpital.*'

As Carla was prepared for the airlift, James explained to Ben that the paramedic had said it wasn't possible to transport him to the hospital with his wife. They had limited access to helicopters and still had to make at least two more emergency calls before returning to the hospital. There was no room for passengers.

He started to prepare Carla for the airlift as James told Ben what the paramedic had said.

'No,' replied Ben, almost shouting in anger. 'I'm going to the hospital with my wife!'

James translated his response, but the paramedic had understood the general direction of Ben's outburst.

'*Il n'est pas!*' he said to James and turned apologetically to Ben. '*Je suis désolé.*'

'I will not let her go on her own. I'm going with her!'

James took command.

'Ben, he says that he's sorry, but you can't go with Carla.'

He turned to the paramedic.

'Will it be possible to get him transported to the hospital some time later today?' James asked in French.

'I've no idea,' the paramedic replied sharply. 'We don't know the extent of the damage to the area, or how many casualties we have. We came straight out to answer this emergency call.'

He turned to Ben.

'I'm sorry, but you can't come with us,' he said firmly in French. 'You have no idea how lucky you were that we could get to your wife so quickly, but I'm afraid I've no idea when, or if, we can transport you to the hospital!'

His radio burst into life: 'What's going on, Henri? Are you ready to airlift up? Over.'

'Almost, I just need to get further information. Over.'

'Well hurry up, Henri! We have an emergency situation in Bargemon and need to get there fast. Over.'

Ben turned desperately to James.

'What's he saying?'

James sighed. 'He said you cannot go with them and they don't know when they can get you to the hospital.'

'I've told you: I'm not leaving her!'

Andrea put her arm around him.

'Ben, you know you have to stay here! We've no idea how much damage the storm has done and they've just said on their radio that they have to go quickly to an emergency in Bargemon. You have to let Carla go and they won't take you because they haven't enough room in the helicopter.'

'Andrea's right: you must stay here,' said James.

The paramedic had now lost interest and patience in the discussion.

'Who owns this place?' he barked in French.

'I do,' said Georges coming forward, ashen-faced.

'Get me this woman's papers immediately,' he ordered and turned back to James. 'Help me get this stretcher downstairs so that I can connect it up for the airlift.'

Georges went off to get the necessary information whilst the paramedic secured Carla on the stretcher. Ben approached him, but Henri was determined not to be delayed any longer.

'*Monsieur, si vous continuez comme ça, j'appellerai la gendarmerie!*'

James came forward and pulled Ben back.

'Ben, he says if you obstruct him again he'll have you arrested. Now back off!'

Ben knew he was defeated. He kissed his wife and watched helplessly as they carried the stretcher downstairs. Georges was waiting for them in the reception and handed over the appropriate documentation. With James's assistance they took the stretcher outside, connected it up and then gave the order for it to be lifted onto the helicopter. He turned to the group of shocked and weary onlookers.

'The police will come tomorrow and take statements,' he told them. 'They'll be able to inform you when you can return to England.'

He then gave orders to be lifted up himself and in the blinking of an eye he and the helicopter were gone.

They all looked at each other in shock.

'Have you heard from your daughter?' Andrea asked Georges.

'Yes, thank God,' he answered wearily. 'She's safe, but there's no electricity and she doesn't know how much damage has been done to the town.'

'Well, that's one good thing,' said Andrea. She suddenly had a thought and turned to James. 'Don't you think somebody had better check up on Sarah? We haven't seen her since we found her wandering around outside our room. I don't know if she took any more sleeping tablets.'

Maria Ribert supplied the answer. 'I looked in on her briefly on the way to Monsieur O'Sullivan's room. She seemed to be fast asleep.'

'You mean she slept through all this?' asked Ben incredulously.

'The hospital told Carla that the sedatives were very strong,' added Maria. 'Perhaps you should take some too, Monsieur O'Sullivan. They're stored in the reception. Carla gave them to me when you returned from Les Baux.'

'No, thank you. I'm going to ring my brother to see if he can use any influence to make the authorities take me to the hospital tomorrow.'

'I'll come inside with you,' said Susan. 'I need to try and get some sleep.'

Once they were safely out of audible range, James asked, 'How the hell does he think his brother will be able to influence the situation here? He's just a regular officer in the army, isn't he?'

'I don't know, but what are we going to do now, sir?' said Michael, when he was quite sure that his wife, Susan, and Ben were out of earshot. 'We can't continue with the operation after this. The British press will be on to the rescue of Carla O'Sullivan in the morning and our cover could be compromised. I knew they shouldn't have been allowed to come!'

'My God,' said Maria in despair. 'What will happen if Foxicat finds out?'

'Everyone calm down,' ordered James. 'We're all tired and shocked and I really think we need to try to get some sleep. However, I agree with you about Carla and Ben O'Sullivan. I'm going to contact London when I get to my room and see if they can arrange for Ben to be airlifted out of here as soon as possible.'

'But James,' protested Michael, 'if CAT is monitoring our signals they'll move in immediately.'

'I'm going to have to take that risk!'

Maria spun round heatedly.

'You can't do that! If CAT suspects anything, they'll kill us!'

James turned on her in a flash of anger.

'Madame Ribert, we cannot compromise the safety of a civilian. We have to get Ben O'Sullivan out of here as soon as possible. Anyway, with a bit of luck the storm will have seriously disrupted their surveillance.'

Michael intervened.

'I don't see what the urgency is, sir. Is there any evidence to suggest that we're in imminent danger?'

James sighed. 'Yes, I think there is.'

He now had their undivided attention.

'Firstly, I believe that Colin Radley was murdered.'

'Whatever makes you say that?' exclaimed Georges.

Michael stared at James.

'Colin died in an accident at a tourist resort. He was blown off the cliff face by a gust of wind. How could he have been murdered?'

'There's something that you don't know. Just before we left England, we received intelligence that suggested Colin's identity had been discovered and that Foxicat had ordered him to be killed.'

They all looked at James in alarm as he continued. 'Two days after we arrived in France, he died. That's too much of a coincidence for me!'

'But there's nothing to suggest he was murdered,' argued Andrea. 'The witnesses all said he'd been caught by an unexpected gust of wind.'

'I'm still not convinced by that story.'

They all stared at him for several seconds. Finally, Michael asked, 'So you think CAT has been watching us for the past two days?'

'Yes, I do; and for that reason I want to have us airlifted out of here as soon as possible, but we must protect the civilians first. If we can arrange for Ben to be transported to the local hospital in the morning, it will just look like the authorities wanted him to be close to his wife.'

'Yes, that's feasible,' said Michael. 'But I'm not sure about us, sir. The General Secretariat won't be able to get substitutions for us at such short notice and we still haven't stopped the consignment.'

'If we've been infiltrated by CAT then we'll need additional protection. If you keep in mind that, in order to avoid suspicion, we've been provided with limited weaponry only and certainly nothing that will stand up to Kalashnikovs. We know CAT have a number of AK-47s in Var and, anyway, if Foxicat suspects that there is any thing dodgy going on here, he'll have already changed the distribution route.'

'So you think we could be ambushed?' asked Michael.

'It's looking increasingly possible, isn't it?'

Maria was dismayed by the change in their fortunes.

'What about us? They'll be able to protect all of you, but what will CAT do to us?'

James turned on her. In the calm after the storm the moon had appeared and the stars were twinkling brightly. In the natural light of the Provençal night, there was no mistaking the ruthlessness in James's eyes.

'Must I remind you that we are all security agents, working to break up the CAT organisation, which is the most dangerous terrorist cell operating in Europe? We know they provided financial support for the training of the 9/11 attacks on America and the Bali bombings. They're now funding a big attack on Britain, probably in London, and they have to be stopped!'

He paused for a moment, before adding callously: 'You and your husband, however, Madame Ribert, are ex-CAT terrorists who are working with us in order to avoid very long prison sentences. We will try to protect you as far as we can but if we fail then you'll only have yourselves to blame!'

The Riberts glared at him, as he continued. 'My priority is to protect the innocent civilians in Britain from a biological attack and that's why I intend to contact the UK National Central Bureau to request assistance.'

He looked at his agents.

'Is there anyone who disagrees with that?'

None of them did and so James went into the building to make his report. For a moment, the remaining British agents observed Maria and Georges contemptuously before returning to their rooms. When they had gone, Maria turned to her husband, frightened.

'Georges, what are we going to do?'

'Die, I think!'

Three

Whilst the agents were discussing their fate, Ben returned to his room and telephoned his brother. Scott listened anxiously to Ben's account of the storm and Carla's hospitalisation.

'What are you going to do, Ben?'

'I was hoping that you might be able to use some of your influence in the army to persuade the police to take me to the hospital. I've no idea what state the roads are in, or even if our car is undamaged, and I'm desperate to see Carla.'

'I'll try, Ben, but I can't promise anything. Would you like me to come out there?'

'Could you? I don't speak the bloody language other than to order a beer or a meal and I felt such a tosser having to rely on complete strangers. I couldn't communicate with the ambulance crew at all!'

'It's not a problem, Ben. I'll contact a guy I know in the Home Office at first light and try to get you some transport. Then I'll organise for my leave to be extended and get straight over to you. Where did you say the hospital was, Draguignan?'

'That's what the paramedic said.'

'I'll ring them later to see if there's any news on Carla. Do you have the number?'

'No Scott. It all happened so quickly I didn't think to ask.'

'Don't worry, I'll get it. Have you got much juice left in your phone?'

'I charged it last night before we lost the electricity and I also have Carla's phone, which I've switched off.'

'Perhaps you ought to switch yours off, too, and conserve the battery.'

'No, I'm not turning it off tonight. If you get any news from the hospital, I'll want you to let me know immediately.'

'OK. Try to get some sleep and I'll call you later. I won't ring Mum and Dad or Carla's parents until the morning. Bye, mate.'

'Bye, Scott, and thanks. Speak later.'

Ben couldn't have any inkling that his conversation with Scott was being listened to by terrorists. Alerted to the impending storm, they had dismantled the surveillance equipment and stored it in a concealed priest tunnel that connected La Maison to Bargemon and Callas. The tunnel was a credit to its original constructors. It followed the route of a major fault in the rock, which formed when the Alps were created over forty million years ago. It was discovered by the original builders of Bargemon and Callas, who carved it into a tunnel, linking the two towns at three entry points. La Maison had been built over one of the exits in the mountain above Bargemon. Now it was used to harbour terrorists and smugglers, rather than to offer an escape route to fleeing Huguenots.

The assassins had taken refuge in the tunnel until the violent tempest had passed and then, as directed by Foxicat, they had crept out and re-installed the monitoring equipment. CAT had received a tip a few months before, alleging the Riberts were double-crossing them; but, contrary to the reports from agents in Britain, they still didn't have proof. As a result of this intelligence, Foxicat had instructed that La Maison be put under twenty-four-hour surveillance. The property had become an important outlet for the notorious terrorist group, Consortium to Aid Terrorism – universally known by the acronym, CAT. CAT had been attracted to La Maison due to its remote location and the unique accessibility through the priest tunnel. The escape route had many cleverly concealed cubby holes in which illegal merchandise could be safely stored before shipment. So CAT were very reluctant to close down the route but knew they would have to if it became necessary.

They listened in carefully to James's request to abandon the operation and organise their safe exit.

'Are you sure we need to do this?' asked London. 'We'll agree to lift out Ben O'Sullivan tomorrow and reunite him with his wife, but the storm must have disrupted their surveillance. You can't be in any imminent danger and, if we move you now, it will confirm everything to CAT.'

'I don't agree, sir,' insisted James. 'The Riberts are very worried that their collusion in this operation has already been discovered by CAT, which will put us all in danger.'

'We know Foxicat is suspicious, but we have no intelligence to suggest that the Riberts' part in this has been uncovered.'

'I do realise that, sir, but I have to confess that I'm also very apprehensive about the sudden death of Colin Radley. I personally feel it's too much of a coincidence that he died at Les Baux, only days after Foxicat had, in effect, issued a fatwa!'

'We've checked it all out, Baker. The French police are quite certain that Radley fell to his death accidentally. He couldn't possibly have been pushed. All the witnesses agree that the closest person to him was his wife. If he had been pushed, then it could only have been her. Are you suggesting that she killed her husband?'

'No, sir,' conceded James, almost laughing as he realised the idiocy of his claim.

'We can't risk losing track of the biological weapons. It has to be stopped, you know that.'

'Are we one hundred per cent sure it's anthrax?'

'The French NCB are. Have you checked the tunnel?'

'Not yet. Michael and I had intended to do it during the night when every one was asleep, but the storm put paid to that!'

'What about the Riberts?'

'They're shit-scared, sir. They'll do whatever we tell them.'

'Good. Although, when all this is over, we might have to provide them with new identities. Search that tunnel as soon as you can and get back to us. I'll organise back-up for you.'

'Very well, sir. We'll reassess the situation in the morning.'

'*Les idiots!*' said the surveillance operator, more to himself than to anyone else.

As soon as the call had finished, he scrambled a direct call to Foxicat.

'What is it?'

'We have just got the proof that Ribert is a traitor.'

He played a recording of the conversation. When it was finished he asked: 'What are your instructions?'

'Wipe them out in the usual way. Make it clear to the authorities that it was us!'

'Very well, sir. One of the guests at the house is not an agent; his wife has been seriously injured and she has been airlifted to hospital. What shall we do with him?'

'Are you sure he's not involved?'

'He's been thoroughly checked out. We've intercepted all his calls and texts. He's a schoolteacher and his brother's in the British army. He has no connection with La Maison and his brother is a translator in the officer corp.'

'What about his wife?'

'She's a chemist and works at a large research laboratory near London.'

'So they are genuinely there on their honeymoon?'

'Yes.'

'Only dispose of him if it's necessary and you can cease his surveillance. Give the order to move in and alert Commander One. He'll meet up with the troops in the tunnel.'

'I'll do that immediately, sir.'

The call came to an abrupt end and the operator sent an encrypted text message to the leader of the operation. The squad were highly organised and on permanent standby, so it wasn't long before they all met up with their commander in the tunnel. After confirming their instructions, they moved swiftly towards the concealed entrance in the reception of La Maison. They entered undetected and went to the pre-arranged rendezvous sites. There were no emotions as they prepared for the attack. The whole team were fanatically committed to their aim of destabilising Western democracies.

Georges and Maria couldn't sleep. James's threatening words were still haunting them. They both knew they had only themselves to blame, but it had been so easy to become embroiled in their lucrative world. When they had secured the property from the church, CAT had approached them with a proposal to fund all the renovations as payment for their collaboration. They had become irreversibly immersed in a web of deceit and it had become impossible to break free. When the security forces had discovered their involvement, they had been blackmailed into cooperation by threat of imprisonment. The alternative to collaboration had therefore become incarceration and confiscation of all their assets. As a result of their deception, the Riberts' multifaceted lives had become even more complex.

'I'm going downstairs to make some coffee,' Georges finally announced to his wife. 'The wood-burning stove should still be hot and, thankfully, the water supply hasn't been cut. Do you want me to bring a cup up to you?'

'Yes please, Georges.'

Georges lit a candle and went out onto the landing. He didn't notice the CAT agents make their move and follow him down into the kitchen. They slunk outside waiting for the right moment to commence the offensive. The opportunity arose as he filled a saucepan with water and placed it on the hob of the stove. Silently, they entered the room and Georges experienced a strange unease, suddenly aware of being watched. He tensed and spun round defensively, but relaxed as he saw a familiar figure illuminated in the firelight. He spoke in French.

'Good evening, or should it be good day?' he joked feebly. 'What are you doing here? I didn't expect to see you for a few days.'

There was no reply.

'Is there something wrong?' he asked, moving closer. 'It's very early in the morning for you to be making an unscheduled visit.'

He was suddenly aware that there was more than one person in the room.

'Are we moving the consignment now?' he asked, puzzled.

'No,' was the reply. 'We've come to deal with traitors.'

'What?' said Georges, as a wave of nausea consumed him.

'We've discovered that you've betrayed us. You and your wife know the consequences of that.'

Georges was horrified – how could they know?

'I don't understand,' he said. 'We haven't betrayed anyone! We've done everything you've asked.'

'We helped to set you up with this hotel business because we knew it would be a good cover for our activities,' snarled the intruder. 'But you've let us down, and now you're going to pay the price!'

'We haven't done anything wrong! I don't understand what you're saying.'

The intruder looked carefully at Georges for a few moments before replying, 'We know the real identity of the guests in your hotel. They're agents for British intelligence and they're working with your cooperation. Foxicat is not pleased!'

'We're not working with anyone,' he persisted, but he knew in his heart that all hope had evaporated away. 'We've been loyal to Foxicat!'

'We've been monitoring all your communications for months and heard the message to London this morning. We know everything.'

Fuck, thought Georges. *We're all dead!* His jaw dropped in fear as he involuntarily soiled himself.

They moved in quickly and Georges saw too late the flash of silver as a cleaver was raised above his head. It was swiped powerfully at a right-angled plane across his throat. Georges didn't have a chance to react. He fell to the floor as blood gushed freely from the severed arteries. As the life force drained from his body, he went into involuntary convulsions. His assailants were on him instantly, hacking away at his arms and legs until they were severed from his body. Eventually, Georges Ribert was relieved from the pain. The spasms stopped and blood oozed gelatinously from the dismembered limbs.

The commander instructed: 'Upstairs and get the others! The woman from the hotel – make her suffer!'

'What about their leader?'

'Make him suffer, too!'

'Excellent. We're obviously in for a good night!'

They put on night vision goggles and crept silently up the stairs towards Maria Ribert's room. The shadow from the moonlight added an even greater menace to their sinister silhouettes. Reaching the door, they heard movement inside and immediately fell back into the shade.

Maria was lying in bed, her anxiety heightening as the time slipped slowly by. Georges hadn't materialised with the promised coffee and this added to her unease, prompting her to wonder what could be delaying him. Finally, unable to contain her curiosity any longer, she got out of bed, picked up the candle on her bedside cabinet and moved towards the door. Her mind began to play games with her as she moved through the soundless dark. What could be keeping her husband?

So completely pre-occupied was she with troubled thoughts that she didn't notice the hidden bodies lurking in the shadows. As she headed for the stairs, the CAT soldiers moved silently behind her – they had clear instructions from their leader and wouldn't hesitate to carry out their heinous task. A rustling sound behind her caused a prickly sensation to run down her spine. She stopped and spun around. The flickering candle in her hand cast distorted images in the dim light, causing the blackness around her to ripple mysteriously. Her heart now started to pound so hard that it was almost deafening in the silence of the night. Beads of sweat trickled down her cool, clammy skin. Tension continued to mount inside her body and she cursed herself for being so jumpy. CAT soldiers, camouflaged perfectly in the darkness, had fallen back out of sight. Maria strained to see what had startled her, but could see nothing – and yet she was sure there'd been some movement.

'For Christ's sake, get a grip of yourself, woman!'

She took a deep breath and made a concerted attempt to pull herself together, but her anxiety was inexplicably increasing.

'Why the hell am I feeling so tense? It's the early hours of the morning and everyone's asleep!'

She looked around nervously but couldn't discern anything out of the ordinary. Her heart continued to thud painfully in the eerie silence and her breathing became more rapid and laboured. Putting one hand over her mouth and rubbing her lips nervously, she thought: *This is my house! There's nothing here to harm me.*

This didn't allay her fears as she turned apprehensively towards the stairs. The wooden steps creaked and groaned as she made her way down towards the kitchen. The candlelight projected a sinister shadow, which occasionally caught her eye, making her violently flinch. On reaching the hall, she stopped and tensed up again, but wasn't sure what had prompted her to come to a standstill. Then she heard the stairs gently squeak behind her and spun around. Still there was nothing to be seen in the blackness. The noise stopped and she almost went back to the stairway to investigate but something intuitively prevented her.

'Why didn't I bring a torch?'

She was sure she had heard the sound again and, on looking up, thought she imagined dense shadows swiftly descending towards her. Fear now overwhelmed her; she panicked and made a sudden dash for the kitchen, dropping the candle as she tripped over the wicker mat in the kitchen doorway.

She looked around the empty room in fright.

'Georges, where are you?' she cried out in a coarse rasping voice. Her mouth, she realised, was dry and she was unable to swallow.

There was no reply. The wood-burning stove afforded a better light than the one she had accidentally extinguished, but it was still dull and inadequate. She heard a sound behind her again and spun around, but the CAT soldiers hung back, hiding in the shadows of the hallway. They watched her with fascination. Their excitement was reaching an almost orgasmic peak. The stalking of their victim was a major part of their job satisfaction and all that remained now was the pleasure of the kill. They could barely contain their excitement as they observed her fear and anxiety. It was all part of CAT's effective programme of instilling terror. They had been ordered to exterminate the British agents quickly, but for the moment, they were enjoying tormenting their helpless prey.

Maria was feeling disorientated as she stood alone in the dim flickering firelight, not even noticing the strong smell of excrement that permeated the room.

'Georges, where the hell are you? I'm frightened!'

She moved over towards the fire and was confused by the stickiness at her feet. 'What the hell am I walking in?'

She bent down to touch the cold stone floor. The surface was wet and tacky to the touch. As she brought the tips of her fingers closer to her face, she stared at them and recoiled in terrified horror.

'My God, it's blood!'

Maria moved closer towards the stove. Her terror was now so great that she didn't even notice the CAT assassins slink quietly into the room and move slowly towards her. She stumbled and picked up the object that had impeded her progress. It was a bloodied dismembered limb. Georges's arm!

Choking back the nausea that now threatened to engulf her, she dropped the limb in abhorrent shock. Seconds later, Georges's severed head rolled towards her, kicked over by one of the malicious murderers. Maria opened her mouth in an attempt to scream, but there was no sound. The terror that had muted her had also rooted her to the spot and she couldn't move.

Suddenly, she was grabbed from behind and felt a sharp pain across her throat. Maria swiftly realised that she couldn't breathe, feeling the blood spill from the gash across her neck. She panicked and tried to shout out again, but her vocal cords had been severed. As her bladder contracted and released urine over the floor, she was dragged towards the kitchen table. A familiar voice whispered in her ear, '*Traître!*'

The pain was now indescribable as she was ferociously reminded of the expertise in fear and torture in which all CAT soldiers excelled. Her suffering was mercifully short-lived, as the massive blood loss dulled her senses and helped kill the pain. She was vaguely aware of being dumped onto the kitchen table and she offered no resistance as she experienced a further burning sensation across her stomach. Maria tried to scream out again but only blood oozed from her mouth. She was barely conscious as the intestines were ripped out of her body and symbolically wrapped around her neck. No longer could she feel the searing burning sensation that had wracked her body and by now all the sounds around her had melded into one mellifluous monotone.

Gradually, Maria became weaker. Strange discordant music permeated her semi-consciousness and through a red mist she could just make out Georges in the distance. He was beckoning to her from the end of a gloomy cavernous tunnel. As she started to move towards him the darkness consumed her and she blacked out.

'Christ, I enjoy that more than sex!' said one of them quietly, laughing as he went over to the kitchen window. He opened the shutter.

'There's still another four to go!' replied another.

They stepped back in satisfaction, enjoying the moment, as they gratifyingly observed the mutilated bodies in the contrasting yellow and blue incandescence of the fire and moonlight.

After the murder of Georges and Maria Ribert, the team were coordinated to attack the remaining agents simultaneously. Three assassins waited patiently outside the other two bedrooms and burst in at the exact same moment. Susan and Michael Chapman were taken completely by surprise and didn't have time to react as they were shot through the head, the sound of the gunfire muffled by silencers. As planned, their lives were extinguished in seconds. They too were mutilated and the assassins carefully wrapped the intestines around their necks.

James and Andrea were lying in bed, neither of them able to sleep. After an eternity of tossing and turning, Andrea sat up.

'We can't sleep so why don't we go and search the tunnel now?'

'Alright. London has verified that it was an accident at Les Baux, so at least we don't have to go there later today.'

'James, I've been thinking about the way CAT operates. Do you think it's possible that the consignment might have been stored here already?'

'No, Ribert would have told me if it was.'

'Would he?'

'Yes, as I told London, he's shit-scared. He knows we're his only hope for survival. The Riberts' days of double-crossing are well and truly over!'

'I don't trust either of them.'

'Nor me. Personally, I would have had them locked away for the rest of their lives, but its expedient at the moment to play along with them.'

He started to get out of bed when he heard an unfamiliar sound outside the door. James looked over, slightly alarmed.

'Did you hear that?'

'What?'

'I'm sure I heard something outside the door.'

He turned on his torch and got out of bed. At that moment the door burst open and three men rushed into the room. James was smacked viciously onto the floor and violently kicked in the head.

Andrea hadn't even had time to react. The third assailant moved swiftly over to her, the glasses giving him perfect vision in the darkness. He shot her skilfully through the eye, killing her instantly.

James, who had been temporarily stunned, didn't have time to react before the two men were upon him. He was pushed face down onto the floor, his half-naked body now vulnerable to attack. Before he could defend himself, one of his attackers pinned him down and a sharp long metal brochette was inserted with surgical precision between the second and third thoracic vertebrae. It was aimed through the vertebral foramen and up into his vertebral canal. Within a few seconds, the pike had penetrated the tissue of the spinal cord, passing through the cervical vertebrae and piercing the lower brain stem cells. It paralysed him instantly and disabled his speech. He was pushed onto his back, his body convulsing out of control as neurones fired in succession. James looked up at his attackers and watched in helpless agony as one of them bent over him and slowly slit his throat. He could feel consciousness slipping away as one of the attackers whispered in his ear, '*Encore, c'est Foxicat qui gagne!*'

James drifted in and out of consciousness. Blood gushed from his throat, gradually reducing cellular respiration, until eventually his body gave in to the attack. The convulsions stopped, the blood began to congeal and James was dead. The assassins looked down at him with arrogant satisfaction and moved over to Andrea's body.

'Mark her like the others.'

They stripped her, cut open the abdomen and skilfully removed the intestines. Her colon and rectum were arranged neatly in the shape of a pyramid in one corner of the room and the ileum was wrapped around her neck. The desecration of Andrea's body was executed in the same orderly efficiency as the murders. Once their task was completed, they began to evacuate the premises.

'What about the others?' one soldier asked.

'They aren't involved. Leave them.'

They began to make their escape, but halted for a few moments on the landing. Clearly visible under Ben's bedroom door was a dull light, which moved around and flickered in the darkness. The soldiers were alerted instantly and turned to their leader.

'He's awake. What shall we do?'

'Nothing. Wait here for a few seconds and see what happens.'

Ben was sleeping restlessly when a noise sounding like an object being dropped in the room next door disturbed him. He woke suddenly and sat up. The room was completely black, except for the intermittent flash from his mobile phone.

James must have dropped something, he thought and lay back down in bed.

He was disturbed again by his mobile phone, which bleeped. He reached out for it and accessed a text message from Scott, which had just been delivered to his inbox.

I'VE RUNG HOSPITAL. CARLA OK & AWAKE. WANTS 2 CU 2MORROW. R U OK? S.

The relief was inexpressible. He pressed speed dial number three, but it wouldn't connect. Ben sighed with irritation and noted he was still connected with the SFR network, but only had one bar of signal strength. He tried again and still couldn't get a line. He went into 'text messages' and re-read Scott's communication before selecting 'reply' and typing:

HAVEN'T GOT A FULL SIGNAL, SO CAN'T RING U. THANX 4 THE TEXT. I'LL RING AGAIN LATER. IF I CAN! B.

Hitting the 'send' key he received the reply 'error sending message'. After three more attempts to send the message, he changed the setting to 'save and send' and noted there was now only a limited service.

'Bloody France! I couldn't live in a place like this. Why do I have signal here sometimes and at other times nothing?'

He got out of bed and wandered around his room, concentrating completely on the bright screen of his mobile phone. There was still no signal. He went over to the bedroom door, opened it and went out into the hall. He was so totally engrossed with his mobile phone, that he was oblivious to anything else going on around him.

'Ah, a signal at last!' he said aloud and pressed 'send'.

'Message sent' displayed on his screen. He smiled in smug satisfaction, totally unaware of the soldiers closing in on him. He looked up and suddenly saw six blacked figures standing in the hall landing, watching and slowly moving closer.

'What the fuck!' he exclaimed.

'*Vous idiot*,' said an unfamiliar voice.

'What are we going to do with him?' asked one of the assassins. 'Foxicat told us not to harm him unless it was necessary.'

'He's seen too much. Kill him!'

They moved in. Ben couldn't understand what was being said; he could only make out the word 'Foxicat', but he realised that he was in great danger. His reaction was instantaneous – he dived into his bedroom and locked the door. With all his strength he forced the heavy dresser across it as the CAT soldiers shot at the door, which disintegrated the lock. They began to barge into the door, forcing it with maniacal strength. Inside, Ben was panicking. Glancing over to the window he could see that it was his only possible escape route. He looked down at his phone, and pressed speed dial in a desperate attempt to contact his brother. Again, there was no signal.

'Fucking phone!' he shouted frantically, accepting that a text message would be his only option.

He quickly typed, 'It was Foxycat', and pressed 'save and send'. To his relief it flashed 'Message sent'. He looked around desperately. They were almost through.

'Ben, you're not going to get out of this one!'

He dived over to the open window and onto his balcony. As he was climbing over the railing, soldiers burst into the room and fired. A bullet hit him.

'Shit! Carla, Scott, I love you!'

He fell and everything went black.

The assassins rushed over to balcony and looked down, their sight enhanced by the night vision glasses. They saw Ben's body crumpled on the terrace below, his head surrounded by a pool of blood. They shrugged remorselessly and left.

Four

Carla sat in the intensive care unit staring at the monitors, along with the array of tubes and leads connected to Ben's body. The emotional trauma of the past few days had taken its toll and she appeared pale and ashen. Her eyes were reddened through frequent attacks of tears and remorse, wishing constantly that she had been with her husband when he had been attacked. When the police helicopter arrived at the hotel to airlift him to the hospital, Ben was unconscious, but he was still breathing. The on-site paramedic decided immediately that there was no treatment he could give the patient at the scene of the crime, so he was rushed to the hospital.

Two days had passed since then and Carla had spent all of her time by Ben's unconscious body. She refused to leave his side, sleeping in the uncomfortable chair by his bed, totally mesmerised by the information flashing and bleeping on the ICU monitors. Hospital staff had stabilised his body and placed him on a ventilator to minimise any further damage. There had been no change in his condition and the doctors were still unsure if he had sustained any debilitating brain trauma. Not knowing the extent of his injuries only added to Carla's unease as she continued her bedside vigil. She was still gazing into the monitor, drifting into a comatose state, when she was jolted by a hand coming down gently on her shoulder. She looked up quickly to see Scott standing over her. Carla jumped up, relieved to see a familiar face and hugged her brother-in-law, before kissing him affectionately.

'Scott! Thank God you're here! When did you arrive?'

'I've just driven from the airport at Nice. I organised a hire car before I left. I'm sorry; I couldn't get an earlier flight.'

'Where are Ray and Janice?'

'Mum deteriorated again last night,' he explained. 'Dad's gone to the hospital with her and is hoping to fly out in a couple of days. He just feels he can't leave her at the moment.'

Scott appeared to be very tired and stressed, his mother's cancer re-surfacing again adding to his misery. He looked over at his brother laid out on the bed.

'How is he?'

Carla sighed despairingly.

'There's no change. He's responding to stimuli but they don't know the full extent of the damage. They've said they might do a CT scan and brain stem-response test later today. That should indicate if any areas of his brain have been damaged.'

'The police in Britain told me that he had been shot.'

'The bullet hit him in the shoulder and it's been successfully removed. The damage occurred when he hit his head on the brick terrace below our bedroom. He must have been trying to escape from his attackers.'

Scott looked over at his brother, went over to him and gently took his hand. Carla joined him and noticed the tears of anger and distress welling in his eyes. He turned to her.

'Carla, why are there two armed special policemen outside this room?'

'I don't know. I assumed they thought Ben might have witnessed something that could identify the attacker.'

'I think it's more than that.'

She looked at him in surprise. 'What do you mean?'

'When I arrived at the airport in Nice I was met by armed police. They had my luggage ready and the keys to my hire car and then they then insisted on escorting me here.'

'They were just being helpful,' said Carla, not very convincingly. 'The police knew you were coming because I told them.'

'But you didn't know my flight number or the actual day I was arriving. When I disembarked, they knew exactly which plane I was on and the name of the hire car company.'

'The French police are very efficient, Scott. Even though I've been through hell and back over the last two days, I've been very impressed with the way they've handled everything.'

He was silent for a moment before saying: 'Carla, I spoke with Ben on the mobile just after you had been airlifted here. They had refused to let him go with you because there wasn't enough space in the helicopter. Ben said they were attending another emergency in Bargemon and they didn't know when they could get him over to the hospital. He asked me if I could use my influence to persuade the police to transport him to the hospital when it was light.'

'The doctors told me that the police had been sent over to La Maison to pick him up. I assumed you had a hand in that.'

'That's just the point. I didn't.'

Carla looked at him, puzzled by his reply. 'Well, who did then?'

'I don't know. When I rang my mate at the Home Office, he said the French authorities had already been instructed by someone in London to pick him up. Not any of the other guests, mind you, just Ben!'

Carla stared at Scott in amazement.

'Also, it was a Priority One request, which means, at the very least, that the Home Secretary and the French interior minister must have been consulted. Now, why would they put themselves to so much trouble for one British tourist?'

'I don't know.'

'I'm sure the French police are very efficient but why did they insist on checking my passport five times at the airport and then another four times in this hospital?'

'Presumably they needed to verify your identity.'

'Obviously! But their thoroughness was ridiculously over the top. Who's in charge of the investigation?'

'Pierre Mauron, he's the chief of police and seems really pleasant.'

'When we have some more news about Ben, I'm going to the police headquarters to see him.'

'He's in the hospital now, attending a meeting with the pathologist.'

'Do you know where the meeting is?'

'No, but I assumed it was in the pathology labs.'

'OK, you stay here with Ben and I'll go and locate him. I'll be back as soon as I can.'

Scott moved over to the door but was prevented from leaving the room by the two guards outside the door.

'Would you mind moving out of the way?' asked Scott in French, politely, but with confident authority.

'I'm sorry, sir, but we can't let you leave this room,' said the officer, equally politely.

'Don't be ridiculous,' answered Scott. 'I want to see Inspector Mauron. I have some questions I'd like to ask him.'

'I'm sorry, sir, but we have our orders.'

Scott was taken aback.

'Are you saying we are prisoners here?'

'No, sir, you're not under arrest.'

'Then please move out of my way so that I can go and speak to the Chief of Police.'

'I'm sorry, sir, but that isn't possible.'

Scott could hardly believe what he was hearing. 'And what will you do if I try to leave this room without your permission?'

'I will have to disable you, sir.'

'What!'

'I'm sorry, but I've been instructed not to let you leave this room unaccompanied, but I'll send a message to Chief Inspector Mauron and inform him that you wish to meet with him.'

'Thank you. Please do it immediately.'

Once again, there was no mistaking the authority in Scott's voice. He went back to Carla, shaking his head in disbelief.

'What did they say?' she asked.

'I'm sorry, I'd forgotten that you don't speak French. He said I couldn't leave this room!'

'What! Did they give a reason?'

'No. Have they let you leave here?'

'I haven't wanted to; they've brought me food and I've slept on this chair.'

'Are you saying you haven't been to the toilet in two days?'

'Of course, but now you mention it I have always been accompanied by someone. I haven't been anywhere on my own.'

'So, in effect, we're under house arrest.'

'Why? We haven't done anything wrong!'

'I don't know, but I'm beginning to think that you and Ben have accidentally stumbled into something big.'

'Like what?'

'I'm not sure – yet! However, I have my suspicions.'

He was about to continue but was interrupted by the guard. The police officer addressed Scott.

'Inspector Mauron will see you after his meeting with the pathologist. Can I get you some coffee whilst you wait?'

'Yes, please,' Scott replied resignedly. 'I haven't had a drink since leaving the plane.'

After the policeman had left, Scott turned back to Carla.

'Have you met the pathologist?'

'No, Scott. He only deals with the dead and Ben is still very much alive.'

Scott looked over at his brother and shuddered.

Pierre Mauron was in the pathology lab discussing the murders with the department controller, Jean-Jacques Broqua.

'Jean-Jacques, are you telling me that these people were tortured before they were killed?'

'Some of them were. Three were shot through the head, but as for the hotel proprietors and one of the other guests...' He stopped, visibly upset by his discoveries. 'God only knows what torment they went through before they died.'

'Is there any evidence of resistance?'

'The forensic data indicates that it was a simultaneous stealth attack. Only the man unconscious in ICU seems to have put up any resistance. I wonder why he was able to defend himself and the others weren't.'

'I've no idea,' said Pierre evasively. 'What about the woman found dead in her bed?'

'Her husband was killed in an accident at Les Baux de Provence the day before the attack. It appears that she overdosed on the sedative Restoril and alcohol.'

'Could she have been forced to take it?'

'The autopsy didn't produce evidence of any violence and her body was in a more advanced state of rigor mortis than the others. That suggests she was already dead when the attack commenced. She exhibited all the classic signs of benzodiazepine poisoning: a sudden reduction in blood pressure resulting in cessation of breathing, coupled with liver and kidney failure. What do we know about her, Pierre?'

'She was French, apparently.'

'Was she? I thought she had a British passport.'

'She obtained British citizenship after her marriage. In fact she was born in the same area of Provence as you, Jean-Jacques. Her father was in the army and she was brought up in the Middle East. She eventually moved to England and it was there she met her husband.'

'Is her body being returned to England?'

'No. The British police informed me her will requests that she's buried in France with her parents – in Draguignan!'

'Really?'

'Yes. Where's the body now?'

'Why? There was nothing more I could do with it here, Pierre, but I have examined her thoroughly. After completing the report, I sent the body from the mortuary to be boxed up by the undertakers.'

'Very well. I'll leave you to make all the necessary arrangements. I suppose she could be buried tomorrow.'

'Alright. I'll organise that at once,' he stopped and thought about the murders for a moment before asking, 'Have you any idea who might have done this and why?

'That stupid journalist who was with the police patrol when they found the bodies is harassing me into making a public statement. He reckons it was a ritual execution carried out by Masons again!'

'Not Paul Barle?'

'Yes, and this time I'm going to have to do something about him. We can't have him stirring up hysteria again!'

'Do you think it was an execution?'

Pierre was silent for a few moments whilst he thought through the pathologist's question. 'You've suggested to me that the implementation of the injuries had been perfectly manipulated.'

'That's right, Pierre. The cutting of Maria Ribert's throat was at exactly the right depth to ensure the nervous system wasn't damaged.'

'What would have been the point of that?'

'I assume it was to guarantee the woman was in the maximum amount of pain before she died.'

'That settles it then. Obviously, this was designed to be a part of some form of elaborate punishment.'

'Punishment! Why would anyone do that?'

'I have no idea, Jean-Jacques, but I intend to find out.'

'Well, if it's not Freemasons, could it be a re-emergence of the coven that you suspect is still operating in the area?'

Pierre stepped back, thinking through the situation.

'We've never been able to prove that; it's still just a theory.'

'From what I can remember, the pattern of some of the mutilations is similar.'

'I don't know, Jean-Jacques, but I'll have to get on to this before we start having trouble with Paul Barle. I'll have to put pressure on his editor again.'

'So we appear to have a bunch of lunatics on the loose once more.'

'It looks that way and that's all we need at the height of the holiday season!'

Jean-Jacques laughed. 'Yes, the tourist board will be pressurising you to find a rapid conclusion to this. What about the man in ICU?'

'It's possible he saw something, but he's still unconscious. The doctors are hoping to carry out tests on him this afternoon, which should indicate the extent of any injuries. His wife is sitting at his side day and night and his brother has just arrived from England. In fact, he wants to see me after this meeting.'

'What are you going to tell him?'

'I've got nothing to tell him, but there isn't any more we can do here. Have you emailed all the reports to me?'

Jean-Jacques nodded.

'OK. I'm going to go and see Monsieur O'Sullivan. Fortunately he's fluent in French.'

'There's just one other thing, Pierre: I can organise the burial of Sarah Radley as you requested, but what about her relatives in England and France?'

'Apparently, there aren't any.'

'Oh. Well I suppose that makes the arrangements easier to organise. I'll get on to it straight away.'

In ICU, Carla and Scott were staring into the monitors when they were interrupted again by one of the guards.

'I've just had a message from Inspector Mauron. He'll see you now.'

Scott stood up and said to Carla: 'Mauron wants to meet; are you going to come?'

'No, I'd rather stay here with Ben. You go and let me know the outcome.'

Scott left and was escorted to an office just outside of the ICU department. Pierre Mauron was waiting for him and, after the introductions were over, Scott asked aggressively: 'Why are we imprisoned in that ward with my brother?'

'You're not under any form of detention, Monsieur O'Sullivan. However, you must understand that your brother is possibly the only person able to identify whoever killed six people in that hotel. We have to make sure he's safe.'

Scott looked at him intently. 'You still haven't explained why I wasn't allowed to leave the room.'

'It was necessary to complete an intensive security check because we're genuinely concerned for your brother's safety. Until we were one hundred per cent sure of your identity, we couldn't allow you to just wander around the hospital.'

'I take it that you're now convinced that I'm Scott O'Sullivan!'

'We sent your picture to British intelligence and they confirmed your identity about an hour ago. I'm sorry that I was unable to speak with you before now but I have been in an important meeting.

'Am I free to leave now?'

'We would prefer you to stay in the hospital tonight, but if you do wish to leave at anytime then I must insist that you have a bodyguard, or let us know exactly where you are going.'

'You don't think Carla and I are in any danger, do you?'

'I'm currently investigating six murders, one attempted murder and one possible suicide – all at the same hotel. You spoke to your brother just before the attack and we have evidence that you received communication from him during it.'

'How do you know that?'

'We've checked your mobile phone records; well, your brother's anyway.'

Scott looked at Pierre carefully and asked bluntly: 'What's Foxicat's involvement in this?'

Now it was Pierre's turn to look warily at Scott.

'I don't know,' he answered eventually. 'The first time I heard of this character was when I read the transcripts of your brother's text messages.'

'You're the chief of police and you've not heard of Foxicat! I find that hard to believe, Inspector. Why haven't you checked it out?'

'I have tried to check it out, Monsieur O'Sullivan,' Pierre replied coldly. 'There is a file referring to Foxicat on the database, but I haven't got security clearance to read it. I've applied for access codes, but so far I haven't received them.'

'I see.'

'I don't think you do and you must realise that I am telling you all this for your own security.'

'My security!' exclaimed Scott, scornfully.

'If we could check your brother's mobile records then so could this Foxicat. That's why we had to be absolutely sure that you really were Major Scott David O'Sullivan of the British Armed Forces Secret Service!'

Scott was taken aback. 'So you know who I really am, Inspector?'

Pierre didn't answer. 'We're assuming that you intend to stay in France until there's definite news about your brother.'

'That is correct.'

'In the circumstances we are prepared to accommodate both you and your brother's wife in a safe police house. You can't stay in the hospital indefinitely and there's a suitable property available on the outskirts of Bargemon. Actually, quite close to the hotel where your brother was staying. We'll have it ready for you tomorrow.'

'How very efficient you are, Inspector Mauron. May I enquire why you're not putting us in a hotel?'

'We need to make sure you are both safe and naturally we will have an armed guard in the grounds of the house at all times. In a hotel it will be less easy to—'

'Keep us under surveillance,' interrupted Scott.

'You must be fully aware of the necessity for us to keep a close watch over you?'

This time it was Scott's turn not to reply. 'I thought Bargemon was badly damaged in the storm.'

'Thankfully the mudslide was quite localised and only a small section of the town was affected; in the end there was minimal loss of life. This is the only safe house available at such short notice.'

'We'll need a telephone and an Internet connection with email.'

'All of that will be provided.'

'I'll go and tell my sister-in-law and see what she wants to do.'

With that, Scott left the room and headed back towards Ben's hospital room. Pierre Mauron watched him thoughtfully.

Scott entered the ward to find Carla very tearful. He grabbed hold of her.

'What's the matter, Carla?'

'Scott, they've just done the tests on Ben.'

Scott took a deep breath, released his sister-in-law and sat down on a chair beside his brother.

'What were the results?'

'The scan doesn't indicate any permanent damage, but they still need to do more tests.'

'What did the brain stem response show?'

'It's slightly out of the normal range, but they think it isn't a problem.'

'Thank God! Can I see the results?'

Scott was sifting through the reports attached to the end of Ben's bed when they were interrupted by one of the doctors. He spoke to Scott in French.

'It's good to meet you Monsieur O'Sullivan. My name is Doctor Labinot Krasniqi and I'm in charge of your brother's recovery programme.'

Scott looked at him gravely.

'What's his situation, Doctor?'

'We think there's a possibility that he could make a full recovery. He had a severe blow to his head and it's miraculous that he's still alive.'

'The O'Sullivan clan are quite a tough bunch, Doctor!'

The doctor smiled. 'Maybe, but the CT scan shows signs of several haematomas, which may have to be repaired by surgery. There are some contusions on the occipital and temporal lobes of the brain that we think could affect his vision, memory and speech. We've carried out an auditory brain stem evoked response test and that shows an inter-aural latency IPL of five point three milliseconds. That's good, because it indicates that there might not be too much damage to the temporal lobe. So, the news isn't all bad, but we won't know the real extent of the damage unless he regains consciousness.'

'What do you mean, "unless he regains consciousness"? Is there a possibility that he won't?'

Labinot Krasniqi looked carefully at Scott. 'He's responding to mild stimuli, so he's not in a state of stupor. The brain stem test indicated that the contusions sustained by the fall may not result in severe traumatic brain injury. If he does regain consciousness, then we'll know the full extent of his injuries.'

'You said his IPL reading was five point three milliseconds. Isn't that quite high? Shouldn't it be between three and four milliseconds?'

'Five point three isn't very high and indicates a slightly slower than normal response time. With the severe head injury your brother sustained, we aren't concerned by that reading. His neurological system is functioning properly and we are expecting the IPL inter-peak to return to normal in a few days.'

'What are you intending to do in the meantime?'

'It will be necessary to keep him stable for a couple of days and, if his IPL returns to normal, we may consider artificially inducing consciousness. At the moment, he's having glutamine and antibiotics to reduce the risk of any infectious complications.'

'Thank you, Doctor.'

'I understand the police are arranging accommodation for you, but tonight I'm afraid all we can offer is a chair in here next to his wife.'

'That will be fine, Doctor.'

He looked over towards his sister-in-law who was looking blankly at them. Once again, Scott had forgotten she didn't speak any French.

'How's Carla?' he asked the doctor.

'She's still in shock after receiving the news of her husband and is suffering from a mild form of traumatic brain injury. There's no sign of any physical damage and we're confident she is making a good recovery. When the police have arranged somewhere appropriate for you to stay, we'll sign her discharge papers and hand her over to your care.'

He paused before advising: 'We would also recommend that, once she's officially discharged, you don't permit her to stay for long periods of time in this ward. She's suffered a tremendous shock and needs rest. We'll give you some sleeping tablets to take with you and I really think you must insist that she takes them.'

'I will.'

The doctor looked over to Carla. 'We've told her all this, but naturally she wants to be close to her husband and, of course, not all of the medical staff speak English. I have to confess that my English hasn't been sufficient to explain all the technical details of your brother's condition. Your presence here should make things a lot easier for all of us.'

'I'll do my best to help out, Dr Krasniqi.'

The doctor nodded and left the room. After he had gone Carla asked anxiously, 'What did he say, Scott?'

'He said that there is more than a good chance that Ben will make a full recovery. He had some damage to blood vessels in the brain that was caused by the blow, but the doctors will be able to repair them quite easily. There is some bruising to some of the cerebral tissue but the brain stem test shows that he hasn't sustained any permanent damage. They're very optimistic about him and if he hasn't regained consciousness in a few days they'll bring him round themselves.'

'Why can't they do that now?'

'Because he needs to rest and they've ordered me to ensure that you do, too.'

'I can't rest with Ben lying here like this.'

'Carla,' said Scott gently. 'You must, for Ben's sake. When he wakes up, he'll need your support and you won't be any good to him if you're totally exhausted.'

'I know you're right, Scott, but it's not easy resting in here.'

'That's why the police are arranging accommodation for us.'

'I'm not leaving Ben.'

'Tomorrow the police will have a house ready for us and we'll go to it, so that you can rest. The hospital will contact us the moment there is any change.'

'Why are they arranging a house for us?'

'I think they want to keep a close watch on me.'

'Why?'

'That policeman knows that I'm not just a regular soldier.'

'How could he know?'

'There are a number of things I need to tell you, Carla, but not in here. I suspect they're listening in to our conversations.'

'My God! What can we do?'

'I think we should ask if we can go out to a restaurant in Draguignan for a meal tonight. I'll be able to tell you everything once we're out of here.'

'I can't leave Ben!'

'Carla, there'll be no change in his state for a couple of days and I think you need a good meal inside you.'

'But I haven't any clothes. They're all at La Maison.'

'I already thought of that! I've brought some clothes from England. Now, I think I need to persuade the armed soldiers outside to let me go down to my car and get them.'

'Soldiers! I thought they were policemen.'

Scott laughed.

'I've been in the army long enough to recognise a soldier, Carla O'Sullivan. Those men are no more regular policemen than you are!'

'Will they let us go?'

'I've no idea, but we can offer to let one of them come with us. I don't suppose you've had a proper meal since the night of the storm.'

'I haven't.'

'Well, I think it's time you had one.'

'OK, Scott. I give in, but I'll need to freshen up before we go.'

'Not a problem. Now, let's see if they'll let us leave.'

Five

Pierre Mauron was sitting in his office speaking on the phone to one of the guards at the hospital.

'They can go into Draguignan for a meal.'

'Very good, sir. What shall we do?'

'Maintain observation at the hospital and suggest to his brother that they go to the Restaurant Moulin de la Foux. Provide him with the necessary directions and offer to arrange a table for them.'

He put the phone down and organised surveillance at the restaurant.

'Now, Major O'Sullivan, we'll see just how good you really are!'

A couple of hours later Carla and Scott O'Sullivan were seated at a table in the Restaurant Etoiles de L'Ange, drinking a glass of Beaume de Venise and eating a bowl of *bourride*.

'I didn't think I would be able to eat anything. My goodness, I'm hungry! Thanks Scott; this fish stew is fabulous, but I don't understand why we didn't go to the restaurant where we had a table booked.'

'I wanted to make sure we could talk without being overheard and the police organising a table for us at the Restaurant Moulin de la Foux seemed just a little too convenient for my liking. Anyway, as it is, we've probably been followed.'

'How do you know?'

Scott shrugged his shoulders. 'Just call it a soldier's intuition.'

'I don't understand what's going on.'

'Nor me, but I can tell you one thing: I don't trust Pierre Mauron.'

'Why? You've only met him briefly.'

'His body language isn't right. I suspect that there's more to him than meets the eye.'

'Like what?'

'It doesn't matter for the moment. Now, Carla, when you were at La Maison did you hear anyone mention Foxicat?'

'No. Why?'

'Just before Ben was attacked, he managed to send me two text messages. The second one read, 'It was Foxicat.' He spelt it wrong, but he must have meant the same Foxicat that I know of. Does it mean anything to you?'

'Not a thing. What would have prompted him to say that?'

'I'm sure he stumbled across something by accident. He'd sent a message a few minutes before the second text, saying he didn't have a full signal and would ring me later. I suspect he experienced a problem sending it and went outside the room. That must have been when he saw the attackers and somehow he picked up the word "Foxicat". His French isn't very good but he obviously heard that name quite clearly. The police in Britain told me that he'd dragged a piece of furniture over the door, but they still managed to smash their way in. He must have been trying to escape through the balcony window when they broke in and shot him.'

'My God! Have you told Pierre Mauron this?'

'I didn't need to. He'd already read the transcripts of our text messages.'

'Christ, Scott! Did you ask him about Foxicat?'

'Yep, and he said he hadn't heard of him until he had read the records of Ben's text messages.'

'Do you believe him?'

'No. He was lying.'

'Bloody hell, Scott! What are we going to do?'

'He indicated that there's a file on Foxicat, but claimed he hadn't been given access to read it.'

'Who is Foxicat?'

'It's the collective name given to the group leaders of a

particularly nasty terrorist organisation known as CAT. I can't say anymore about it in public – it might not be safe – but when we're in the house I'll fill you in with all the details.'

'I don't understand why Pierre doesn't have access to the file.'

'Neither do I. Perhaps the authorities suspect him of something untoward. Anyway, tomorrow we'll be accommodated in this house in Bargemon with full Internet access. I can then call up the file and see if it answers any of our questions. I was intending to look it up before we left, but then Mum fell ill again and I had to support Dad.'

'How are you going to do all this without Mauron knowing?'

Scott grinned and picked up his mobile phone from the table.

'This isn't just a fashion accessory, you know,' he said. 'I've come prepared.'

Carla laughed nervously and as they continued with their meal a man in plain clothes entered the restaurant. He didn't look over towards them, but sat at the bar opposite their table and ordered a drink. Scott glanced over and smiled to himself. *These bloody amateurs,* he thought. *Will they never learn? I mean, it's so fucking obvious you're watching us!*

'I think we have company,' he said to Carla.

'What?'

She was about to look up, but Scott kicked her shin sharply under the table.

'Don't look over there,' he instructed. 'Our surveillance has arrived. It didn't take them long to catch up with us. Mauron is obviously very efficient!'

'What are we going to do?'

'We'll casually finish our meal, then pop into a bar and eventually stroll back to the hospital. Then, tomorrow we'll go with the police to the house in Bargemon.'

'I'm not happy leaving Ben. I think you should go and leave me at the hospital.'

'That's out of the question! I've read the hospital notes thoroughly and I'm convinced there won't be change in Ben's current state. There's no point just sitting at his bedside; you must have a proper rest.'

Carla knew she was defeated and finished her meal.

As Scott had predicted, there was no change in Ben's condition overnight and the next day Carla reluctantly left the hospital. Pierre Mauron arrived at just after nine o'clock in the morning and escorted them to Pimaquet, the police house on the outskirts of Bargemon. They followed his unmarked police vehicle in Scott's hire car and both experienced a feeling of intense trepidation as they left the main road from Draguignan to Grasse and entered the narrow mountain road leading to Bargemon.

Travelling through the small town of Callas, they were genuinely surprised by the lack of damage. The streets and buildings had been hosed down and most of the residents had moved back to their homes and were in the process of drying out the flood damage. The effect of the storm on the surrounding landscape, however, was clearly evident. Pylons and telephone wires had all been felled and there were construction engineers everywhere attempting to reconnect the surrounding villages with electricity and telephone lines. Rocks were strewn randomly over open countryside and, across parts of the terrain, the force of the water had cut deep ruts into the land. They navigated the remainder of the route in silence. As they moved closer to Bargemon, the number of rocks, lying congruously along the route noticeably increased and the sheer scale of the destruction to the landscape was frighteningly obvious. They turned another sharp corner and in front of them, innocently perched on the side of a jagged outcrop, was Bargemon. The road had taken a sharp arc to the right, leaving a steep drop between the road and the town that afforded them a clear view of the medieval village perched on the mountainside.

'That's Bargemon,' said Carla.

'Isn't it one of the most beautiful places you have ever seen?'

'Yes. That's what Ben said when we first arrived here.'

As they passed through Bargemon, they noticed the inhabitants had already begun to repair the damage and it wouldn't be long before there was little evidence that there had ever been a mudslide. The authorities had cleared some of it away and had repaired the majority of damage to the access road. They trailed Pierre through the main narrow street of the eleventh-century village and passed a café adjacent to a fountain. There, they drove out of the main section of the town and back onto the mountain road, which swung round sharply to the left. Less than a kilometre outside Bargemon, they followed Pierre through a narrow entrance into a rough, narrow drive. The sign bearing the house's name, 'Pimaquet', was barely visible behind a large, woody rosemary bush. The driveway ended at a small house, nestled amongst olive groves and sheltered by trees. Neither the vegetation nor the house appeared to have been damaged.

'Welcome to Pimaquet,' said Pierre, as he unlocked the front door. 'You'll find it very comfortable and we managed to get the mains electricity supply reconnected this morning. We've also transferred all of Madame O'Sullivan's possessions from La Maison and placed them in one of the bedrooms.'

'What about a telephone?'

'The telephone line was connected yesterday and, as promised, you have access to the Internet. The swimming pool has been cleaned and maintained, so there's nothing you need to do. One of my officers will show you around and acquaint you with the running of the property.'

'Thank you, Inspector.'

Pierre looked at him impersonally as he added: 'There will of course be a guard on duty in the grounds twenty-four hours a day.'

'This is for our protection, of course.'

'Naturally, Major O'Sullivan.'

'Are we permitted to leave the house without permission?'

'You are free to come and go as you wish, but we think it prudent to keep a guard posted here.'

Scott turned on Pierre.

'Are you sure you don't know what Foxicat is, Inspector Mauron?'

Pierre looked frostily at Scott, but his eyes betrayed nothing.

'I told you yesterday, Major O'Sullivan, I had never heard of Foxicat until I read the name on one of your brother's text messages. We were unable to access yours.'

Scott concealed a conceited smirk and asked: 'Just out of interest, where exactly is La Maison from here?'

'It's more or less directly above you. The water current was split in two by a rock formation immediately above the hotel and that saved this property, along with much of Bargemon, from total devastation. The access road was washed away and won't be repaired for a few days, so I wouldn't try getting over to La Maison. The terrain is still very dangerous.'

There was hint of a threat in Pierre's voice that didn't go unnoticed by Scott.

'Well, Inspector, I'm sure you have a great deal to do. Our guard will be more than capable of showing us around the house.'

Pierre nodded politely at them and went off with his two police officers. As he was getting into the car he said quietly:

'*La relève de personnelle sera dix neuf heures. Me signalez de suite tous que vous avez trouvé.*'

'*D'accord.*'

Pierre looked up and, to his irritation, he observed Scott watching him. He had obviously heard every word. He nodded an acknowledgement to Scott, who returned the gesture dispassionately.

After an extensive guided tour of the property by the police officer, Scott and Carla unpacked in their respective rooms and sat by the swimming pool sipping a glass of chilled rosé wine.

'The place seems to be well stocked with food and drink,' observed Scott. 'It's almost as if they don't want us to go out.'

'I didn't follow everything that you said to Pierre, but it didn't sound as if you were being very polite to him.'

'No, I wasn't. The problem is that I don't trust him and he doesn't trust me. It should make for quite an interesting working relationship. Who said *entente* isn't dead?'

'What the hell's going on?'

'I'm not quite sure. So let's go and find out shall we?'

He got up and started to move into the house. Carla followed.

'What are you doing?'

'I'm going to locate that file on the Internet.'

'What about the policeman outside?'

'Soldier,' corrected Scott. 'He won't come into the house and, anyway, even if they're monitoring our use of the Web, they won't be able to break through this.'

He got out his mobile phone.

'What are you going to do with that?'

'I'm going to use it to connect this computer to the Ministry of Defence server. It'll scramble everything we access, so that no one will be able to break into it or know what we're looking at.'

'But it's just a mobile phone, isn't it?'

'No, Carla. This is top-notch twenty-first century technology, provided courtesy of the Pentagon – well, via Thailand, I expect!'

She laughed genuinely for the first time since her hospitalisation.

'Scott, you're an idiot!'

He wasn't listening. He had taken a lead out of a bag and connected one end to his mobile phone and the other to a spare USB port in the computer. A box came up on the screen and he clicked on the 'initialise' icon. The screen went blank and was eventually replaced with the Ministry of Defence logo. He typed in his user name and password – it then asked, 'Who's your favourite person?' Scott typed in the response.

Carla laughed as she saw three asterisks appear on the screen and said: 'Three letters. Let me see; could that be Ben?'

Scott smiled. 'Maybe.'

The programme instructed: 'Please verify your favourite person', to which Scott replied, 'George.' The screen flashed and blinked and within thirty seconds he was in the Ministry of Defence search engine.

'You typed six letters; what were they?'

'You'd need to know the name of my pet tortoise when I was a small boy.'

Carla laughed again. 'You're a genius, but that code doesn't look too difficult to break.'

Scott looked up at her and smiled. Suddenly, Carla thought she was looking at Ben. It was a strange feeling.

'There's one more thing to do, but it isn't activated until I ask it to find something. Now, let's find Foxicat!'

He typed 'Information on Foxicat' in the search engine tool box and waited for a response. It didn't take long before a prompt box came up:

VERIFYING IDENTITY OF MAJOR SCOTT DAVID O'SULLIVAN, SPECIAL OFFICER 5903. RANDOMLY CHOOSING VERIFICATION PROCEDURE.

'Oh dear, it'll be just our luck if it wants my penis girth today,' he joked.

'It had better not!'

Scott laughed.

VERIFICATION POINT 6 REQUIRED FOR USE OF SERVER TODAY.

'What a shame!'

TWENTY SECONDS FOR VERIFICATION 6.

The mobile phone bleeped and Scott placed the tip of his left thumb onto the infrared panel of his phone. He moved it upwards to the first joint, ensuring his thumb print was thoroughly scanned. The phone bleeped and an installation box appeared on the computer screen. It read:

SCANNING.

There was a few seconds of inactivity before the prompt appeared.

VERIFICATION SUCCESSFUL. PROCEED.

He pressed the return key and 'What information do you require on Foxicat?' came up on the VDU. Scott typed in, 'identity'. They stared at the screen for what seemed an eternity before the reply: 'Which Foxicat?'

'Bloody hell, Scott! This isn't any better than the search engine I use at home!'

'Have patience. You're as bad as Ben.'

Carla smiled as he typed in 'List Foxicats'. A long list came up:

FOXICAT ALBANIA

FOXICAT ALGERIA

FOXICAT ANGOLA

FOXICAT ARGENTINA

FOXICAT AUSTRALIA

FOXICAT AUSTRIA (NEE DEUTSCHE)…

Scott scrolled down the list until he found the entry he wanted. He clicked on 'Foxicat France' and the information he wanted came up on the screen.

'Here we are. This should answer your questions, Carla.'

He read it out aloud:

Foxicat is the collective name for the leader in each country of the terrorist group known as CAT. The aim of CAT is to destabilise Western democracies with the intention of undermining democratic governments and bringing an end to world globalisation and capitalism. CAT is suspected of providing the majority of funding for the attack on the United States of America on 11th September 2001, the Bali explosions, attacks in Madrid and the suicide bombings on 7th July 2005 in London. They operate in most Western countries, facilitating the distribution of arms to all the major terrorist groups, along with Class A drugs. They are considered by the International Criminal Police Organisation (ICPO) to be the most dangerous and influential terrorist organisation currently operating. Foxicat France is believed to be based in the South of France, but the identity is unknown. It is believed that CAT has infiltrated the French internal security services and French intelligence is currently cooperating with and working closely with international police and intelligence services.

Scott came to the end of the file and sat back. 'I've been caught up in Middle Eastern politics for the last couple of years, so I've lost track of terrorist groups in Europe. I hadn't realised that CAT had infiltrated the system to this extent!'

Carla was silent for a moment. 'Find out about the link between Foxicat and La Maison.'

The information came up almost immediately. Once again, Scott read it out aloud:

Operation CAT at La Maison has now been aborted, but it has long been known that the property in Bargemon, Provence, known as La Maison, is the centre of a highly organised international drug and weapons syndicate, operated by CAT…

Scott continued to read out the rest of the report and they learned of the consignment of biological weapons that had been purchased in Iran and would be stored in the tunnel beneath La Maison. It was thought that the deadly cache was destined for the United Kingdom in order to perpetrate an attack on London in 2006.

He stopped reading for a moment. 'This adds a new light to things, doesn't it?'

Carla stared at the screen in disbelief.

'Do you mean to say that we booked into a hotel that is at the centre of international terrorism?'

'It looks that way.'

'You don't seem surprised.'

'Well, to be honest, Carla, I suspected something like this. When I received the news about Ben, I continually thought about his last message to me. If Foxicat was involved, then it had to be linked to some form of terrorist activity. Then I arrived in Nice and the police were waiting for me. That, coupled with soldiers guarding Ben, just confirmed my suspicions.'

'What involvement do you have with CAT?'

'Anyone working in the intelligence services has been involved with CAT at some point. As soon as I learned that Foxicat was directly involved, I realised it was serious.'

'So, that's why you agreed so readily to us being moved into this house.'

Scott smiled.

'There were two reasons. Firstly, I needed a private Internet link and secondly, I wanted to ensure you were safe. As soon as I saw those guards, I thought you might be in danger.'

'What about Ben?'

'He's being well looked after. I witnessed that for myself. They won't risk anything happening to him; they're too concerned about what he might have seen.'

'So what are we going to do now?'

'We need to look up the full details of this operation at La Maison. It's obvious to me now that the people killed in the hotel were British agents and somehow CAT broke their cover.'

'My God!'

Scott wasn't listening; he was back on the keyboard attempting to access further information. He typed: 'Operation CAT at La Maison August 2005'.

ACCESS DENIED.

'Fuck! They're onto me!'

Carla was beginning to panic. 'Who are onto you?'

'The NCB in Britain. I'll need to send a priority email.'

'What's the NCB?'

'The National Central Bureau – they're the local offices of Interpol in each participating country.'

'How are you involved with Interpol? You're a soldier.'

'I'm linked to them through my position in the army.'

He clicked on the email icon on the screen and accessed his mailbox. He selected contact one and typed: 'I need to access the file on Operation CAT at La Maison August 2005. 5903.'

The reply was almost instantaneous.

THE ACCESS CODE WILL BE SENT TO YOUR MOBILE. CONTACT US ONCE YOU HAVE READ THE FILE.

Carla stared at the screen as Scott's mobile bleeped.

'What the hell's going on?'

'It appears that I've just been recruited onto an operation. Obviously that consignment hasn't been stopped,' he answered, grimly.

'And they expect you to do it!'

'I'm afraid so.'

He typed in the newly-acquired access code and the file was released from the central data bank.

'Now, let's find out who these people were and what they were doing.'

He called up the file, Operation CAT – La Maison – August 2005, and they both read it in solemn silence. Scott looked up at Carla as they read the section explaining that she and Ben had been allowed to continue with their reservation because the NCB were concerned that CAT was monitoring Georges Ribert's booking system. He could see from her body language and facial expression that she was very distressed and said, 'Hmm. It all seems so different when you are reading about yourself, doesn't it?'

Carla looked up at him, red-eyed and shocked.

'Yes, it's all so cool and clinical.'

Scott shrugged his shoulders.

'It has to be. This is an official report; there's no place in it for emotion.'

'I suppose not.'

'So I was right. The other guests were British agents and it sounds as if they weren't happy about sharing the hotel with you and Ben. Coupled with that, they think CAT has infiltrated the police force in Var, so that would explain a few things. I told you there was something suspicious about Mauron.'

'You're making a huge assumption!'

'Yes, that's what I'm paid to do. Now, we know the Riberts were press-ganged into cooperation with the General Secretariat and the consignment they were trying to stop was anthrax. I wonder how much their daughter knew.'

'Christ, Scott! How could this happen?'

'It's standard practice of the General Secretariat.'

'You used that term just now; what exactly is it?'

'It's the international headquarters of the NCB. Their offices are in Lyon.'

He sat back and considered everything they had just read. 'Files of this nature are updated hourly. Let's see what the latest information is, shall we?'

'I don't know that I want to!'

Scott read out the final sequence, his voice quivering slightly as he read the description of his brother's attempted murder. After he had read the remaining details of the file, he turned to Carla.

'So, the agents were all executed and intelligence service is hoping Ben saw something that could identify the attackers.'

He paused, desperately trying to make some sense of what they had just discovered.

'Carla, tell me everything you know about this woman who they think committed suicide.'

She shook her head. 'Her name was Sarah Radley and her husband had fallen off the cliff at Les Baux. If you remember, Ben told you about it. The hospital gave her sedatives to calm her down and assist sleep.'

'What else do you know about her?'

'Nothing. The woman died just over twenty-four hours after I'd met her.'

'But, you went with her to the hospital after her husband was killed.'

'Scott, when I was with her she was either screaming, crying hysterically or unconscious in the back of our car!'

'Don't you think that seems to be rather unusual behaviour for the wife of a special agent?'

'No, I don't think her behaviour was unusual at all. She'd just seen her husband fall off a bloody cliff!'

Scott once again was only half-concentrating on Carla's reply, as he considered all they had learned. He tapped the desk in front of the computer loudly.

'Restoril, she was prescribed Restoril. Isn't that temazepam?'

Carla nodded.

'What do we know about temazepam?'

Carla provided the answer.

'It's the generic name for a commonly-used sedative of the benzodiazepine group, frequently prescribed as a substitute to barbiturates. It's used for the treatment of insomnia and works by slowing down the metabolic rate. In high doses it can lead to kidney and liver failure and, coupled with the presence of alcohol, it can cause breathing disorders and low blood pressure. Is there anything else you need to know?'

Scott laughed. 'Of course, for a moment I had forgotten you were a research chemist. I wonder what prompted the histrionics.'

'Umm, let me see – witnessing her husband being killed!'

Scott smiled at her sarcasm and replied: 'She was the wife of a senior special agent and, in my experience, such people aren't prone to hysteria or suicide. Also, her body wasn't mutilated like the others, was it? I wonder why. I'll need to see the pathology report on her death.'

'Well, break into the system. It can't be that difficult.'

'It's not, but that could be dangerous at this point.'

'Dangerous?'

'Yes, because we don't know to what extent CAT has infiltrated the French system. We can't risk exposing ourselves at this stage. I'll have to check with London to find out what they want us to do.'

'Can't you use your phone, like you have with the other files?'

'Only using the correctly-scrambled codes. Otherwise, it could be traced.'

He turned back to the VDU and typed another email.

I HAVE READ THE FILES. PLEASE ADVISE.

Once again, the reply was rapid.

LOCATE THE CHEMICAL WEAPONS AND IDENTIFY FOXICAT. PRIORITY ONE. AN AGENT WILL CONTACT YOU IN TIME. USE CODE PHRASE 5D.

As Scott shut down the link Carla asked, pale faced: 'What are you going to do?'

'I am assuming for the moment that our guard will stay in the grounds of Pimaquet. So, we're going to drive down to Bargemon and have a drink in the bar.'

He winked at Carla and said no more.

Half an hour later, they had driven into Bargemon and, after parking the car by the post office, they walked to the Pierrot Taverne Auberge. Scott ordered the drinks, then popped over to the tabac opposite the bar and bought an ordinance survey map of Bargemon. Carla watched him impatiently as he pored over the map. Eventually all her patience was spent.

'Scott, are you going to tell me what you're doing?'

'I'm locating La Maison,' he replied without looking up.

'I can tell you where it is. I was staying there!'

'Yes, but you only accessed it from the road, which Pierre Mauron said had been washed away and, anyway, I don't want the guard at Pimaquet to see us.'

'How do you know we haven't been followed here?'

'I don't, but I'm prepared to take the risk on this occasion. If by some chance we're apprehended, we'll just claim that we wanted to see the place where Ben was injured.'

'So we're going to La Maison this afternoon?'

'Yes, but first I think we should have some lunch. Do you fancy a plate of snails?'

Carla laughed.

'OK and what about a bottle of Chardonnay?'

'A glass! We need clear heads for this afternoon.'

Scott ordered the lunch and, as soon as they had finished, Carla followed him down into the lower section of the town. They climbed over a low wall and made their way through the rough undergrowth in the direction of La Maison. He was able to use the map to negotiate small footpaths, which eventually led up to the road several metres above Pimaquet. As Pierre had informed them, the road had been badly damaged by the storm, but it appeared to have been made passable. This enabled them to carefully navigate the driveway of La Maison. They made their way towards the house, which Carla noted was no longer surrounded by pine trees; most of them had been flattened by the storm. As they approached, there was an unexpected sudden cold gust from the Mistral, which for a second, unnerved them both. However, on looking up at the building, everything appeared to be serene and tranquil. Scott noticed that the front door was open. He put his hand on Carla's shoulder and stopped her moving forward.

'That's odd. The police wouldn't have left the front door open and there's no sign of any cars or anything else around.'

'Surely there can't be anyone here?'

Scott was taking no chances and went straight into military mode. He took a gun from his small rucksack and began to stalk up to the front door. Hearing a sound inside, he quickly concealed himself adjacent to the door and beckoned Carla to keep out of sight. As the sound came closer, he tensed. Eventually, a lone individual emerged on the wooden decking and Scott, well hidden, was able to launch himself effectively on his unsuspecting prey, who was a young woman. He clasped the disabled victim tightly, holding one hand over the mouth and with the other he aimed a gun at her head.

'Don't move or say a word!' he ordered.

At this point, she offered no resistance, terrified by her ordeal.

Carla suddenly recognised the captive. 'For goodness' sake let go of her! It's Monique Ribert! Her parents owned this hotel.'

Scott loosened his grip, enabling Monique to struggle like a wildcat to free herself, but he continued to hold her firmly. In a desperate effort to secure her freedom, she made an unsuccessful attempt to bite his hand, then she saw Carla and began to simmer down. As she gradually cooled off, he allowed her to speak, but this only encouraged her to resume the struggle. She shouted out, insisting that he release her immediately, prompting Carla to repeat her earlier instruction. Scott complied and allowed her to move away. Once free, Monique dashed away from her attacker, shook herself down and glared at Scott before turning to address Carla.

'Madame O'Sullivan, what are you doing here?' she said with relief, but obviously much shaken from the assault. 'I heard that you had been taken to the hospital before all this happened. How are you?'

'I'm fine, Monique.' She gestured in mild embarrassment towards Scott. 'This is my brother-in-law, Scott O'Sullivan.'

Scott nodded an acknowledgement, sheepishly. Monique looked him up and down and regained her composure.

'I can see the resemblance. He and your husband, how do you say in English, are like two peas in a pod?'

Carla laughed. 'Yes, that's the right expression.' She went over to Monique and clasped her hands sympathetically. 'I was so sorry to hear about your parents.'

Monique looked down towards the ground desolately.

'Thank you. I'm sorry about you husband too.'

She looked up at Scott.

'What are you doing here?'

'We came to see where Ben was attacked,' answered Carla.

'I hear you're staying at Pimaquet and that your brother-in-law is in the British army.'

'How do you know that?' demanded Scott, his suspicions instantly aroused.

'My boyfriend's a police officer in Draguignan. He was off-duty on the night of the storm and I was staying at his apartment in Bargemon, but he's heard quite a lot about you since returning back to work.'

'What exactly has he heard?'

'That you're some form of special agent and Inspector Mauron has given you the use of the police accommodation at Pimaquet.'

Scott looked irritated and snapped: 'Mauron's department shouldn't be so loose-tongued! However, it does explain why there have been so many security breaches. Anyway, I'm only here because my brother is lying unconscious in ICU.'

Monique looked at him cynically. 'I'm sure that's the case, Monsieur O'Sullivan.'

Carla intervened. 'Look, Monique, I want you to call me Carla and this is Scott.'

Monique smiled gratefully at them. She went over to Scott.

'Scott, I don't care why you're here. I just want you to find out who killed my parents.'

Scott didn't answer. He put his pistol back into the rucksack and went over to her.

'The attackers gained access through a tunnel. Do you know where it is?'

'Of course I do!'

'Can you show it to us?'

'Yes. Do you have a torch?'

'Of course I have!'

Monique laughed for the first time since her parents had been murdered.

The access to the tunnel was concealed behind a wooden panel in the downstairs hall. It was operated by activating a hidden mechanism in a panel adjacent to the entrance. There was a slight clicking sound and the wooden panel slid silently open. Carla looked into the uninviting black hole that had materialised in front of her, and suddenly was desperate to remain on the surface. However, the thought of staying alone in the close proximity of the attacks was an even more dismal prospect. Scott looked over, sensing her hesitation.

'Come on, Carla. We need to see exactly where this leads,' he said gently.

She nodded an acknowledgement nervously and reluctantly followed him into the dark abyss.

The tunnel led steadily downwards for several metres before levelling off. Carla shuddered as she moved further into the depths of the mountain. With the only illumination coming from Scott's torch, it was frighteningly dark and very damp. Every footstep echoed around them and the oppressive, claustrophobic environment made Carla want to scream out. She fought hard to suppress her anxiety and kept close to Scott, wanting to hold him tightly as they moved further into the blackness. It took about half an hour to reach the first set of stone steps, which led up to the church in Bargemon. Scott stopped and carefully inspected the exit. Carla watched him, but was reaching the point when she could no longer conceal the mounting hysteria which was increasingly overwhelming her.

'Scott, can we go back now? I hate it down here; it's so creepy!'

'We'll go back shortly, Carla. I need to see more of this passage way first.'

Carla took a deep breath and bravely followed him further along the tunnel, which narrowed even more as they moved closer to the town of Callas. It took another twenty minutes to navigate the last segment and Carla's fear became more intense as the walls tapered inwards and confined her further. To her relief, the final section, which originally led to the sea, had been sealed off and their exploration came to a sudden halt.

Scott was studying the barricade when Monique accosted him with the demand: 'I want you to find Foxicat and kill him!'

He looked slightly taken aback. 'How do you know about Foxicat?'

'I'm not stupid. I know what my parents have been doing over the years, no matter how hard they tried to conceal everything from me.'

Scott didn't answer. He was still very unsure of Monique Ribert.

'Also, those people who were murdered with my parents: they were British agents, weren't they?'

'I don't know what you mean.'

'Oh yes you do, because you're one of them as well.'

'And what makes you think that?'

'You held a gun at my head, if you recall. Where did you get it from?'

For one brief moment, Carla forgot her claustrophobia and was able to ask: 'That's a good point. How did you get it through the security check at the airport?'

'Sometimes you can be very naive, Carla. It's simple. It's chipped with a device which confuses the detectors.'

Carla stared at him in disbelief and asked, 'What about all the checks on hand luggage?'

Scott laughed and replied condescendingly, 'Oh Carla! I have diplomatic immunity. No one's allowed to check my hand luggage!'

He turned his attention back to Monique. 'Why do you think the guests in your parent's hotel were special agents?'

'Mama and Papa were becoming increasingly agitated as the time came closer for them to arrive; in the end they couldn't hide it from me. I knew there was something going on, so on the first night of their stay I followed two of the men out in the grounds and I overheard their conversation.'

'So you know that your parents were terrorists working for Foxicat?'

Monique hung her head in shame. 'Yes.'

'Do you know who Foxicat is?'

'Only a handful of carefully-selected people are aware of his identity, but I do know that he's very influential in Var.' Monique looked at him desperately. 'Scott, CAT agents have been using this tunnel for years to store their merchandise. There must be some clues to be found down here and when you find them I want you to kill Foxicat for what he's done to my family.'

The sheer force of her emotion finally persuaded Scott that she might be genuine.

'I'm not an assassin! My job is to bring him to justice.'

Carla wasn't listening to the conversation. The stifling surroundings had finally become too much to bear and she looked over at Scott, realising that she couldn't contain the nausea for a second more.

'Scott, I have to get out of here. I'm scared shitless!'

He turned and caught hold of her; she was shaking and he realised that she was at the end of her tether.

'I'm sorry you're so frightened, but I needed to look down here. We can go back now.'

'Thank God! I can't stay in this freezing hellhole any longer.'

Scott took her by the hand and they moved back towards the hotel. Just before the barricade was out of sight, he turned and looked back, deciding to return later that night and explore it thoroughly himself. If there was an overlooked clue to be found in the subterranean passageway, he was determined to find it. He also wanted to study the bricked-up wall. There was something about it that was vaguely familiar. For the moment, he couldn't think what it was, but he was sure it would come back to him.

They moved back through the passage swiftly and within forty minutes had returned to the entrance hall of La Maison. Carla ran out into the welcome light of the hall, whilst Scott scrutinised Monique carefully as she activated the mechanism to reseal the tunnel. He watched it slide shut and suddenly felt uncomfortable, sensing that someone was watching him. He spun round as a familiar voice asked: '*Bonsoir, Major O'Sullivan. Est-ce que vous avez trouvé quelque chose?*'

Scott was taken aback to be confronted by Pierre Mauron, but as a trained soldier he remained cool and asked the inspector casually what he thought there might be to find in the depths of the mountain. '*Je ne sais pas, Inspecteur Mauron. Qu'est qu'il y a à trouver?*'

'You can speak French!' declared Monique, interrupting the brief exchange between the two men.

'Yes.' He turned back to Pierre. 'You did say that we were free to come and go as we like.'

'I did. Have you found anything unusual in your visit here?'

'Not yet.'

Pierre sighed. 'No, and you won't, either. Our forensic team have studied everything very carefully. There were no fingerprints that couldn't be accounted for and we studied all traces of hair, fibres and blood samples throughout the building. They all matched up with the victims. Whoever perpetrated this attack covered their tracks perfectly.'

'There's no such thing as a perfect crime, Inspector.'

'I hope not and I trust that you're going to help us with this enquiry. I've been hearing some very interesting reports about you.'

'Such as?'

'I've been informed that you were the agent responsible for finding and securing the release of the two French journalists held captive in Baghdad last year. That must have been a tricky operation to realise under very difficult circumstances. Anyway, the Interior Ministry have ordered me to work with you on this case.'

'That makes for a very interesting alliance, Inspector. I'll do my best. Have you been given access to the file yet?'

'No. It's more complicated than I first thought. I have to get an access code from the NCB in Lyon and it looks like that might take some time.'

'When you do finally have access, perhaps you could let me know?'

Pierre didn't answer the question. 'The section of the road leading down to Bargemon has been made passable, but is still closed to general traffic, so would you like us to give you a lift back to Pimaquet?'

'No thank you, Inspector. We'll walk. Anyway, we need to collect my car from Bargemon.'

'As you wish.' He turned to address Monique. 'Mademoiselle Ribert, can we transport you back to Bargemon?'

'No. I'd rather walk back with Scott and Carla.'

Pierre looked at Scott impersonally, nodded and then left with his police officers. After he had gone, Carla joked: 'So, how do you feel about working with Pierre Mauron?'

'I don't know. It depends on how things work out.' He turned to Monique. 'Is it possible to have a spare key to La Maison? I'd like to come and have a look around again tomorrow morning.'

'You can borrow these,' she said, reaching into her pocket. 'I have a spare set back at the apartment.'

With that, they secured the property and made their way back to Bargemon. As they walked down the rough road in the hot Provençal sun Scott asked: 'Just for the record, Monique, which department does your boyfriend work in?'

'Andre works in Pierre Mauron's office.'

Scott looked at Carla sceptically. 'Why am I not surprised?'

Six

Later that night, Scott was wide awake in bed. The time dragged at a snail's pace whilst he waited patiently until he was sure Carla would be fast asleep. After returning from Bargemon, Scott had cooked their supper and they had relaxed over a leisurely meal, discussing the incredible events of the day. Scott knew Carla was both mentally and physically exhausted so, after failing to persuade her to take some sedatives, he had deliberately plied her with alcohol in the hope it would encourage her to sleep. As he lay in bed, with only the sound of cicadas for company, his mind was functioning in overdrive. He had already decided to return alone to La Maison after dark and attempt to access the concealed storage areas, which he was sure were located throughout the length of the tunnel. Scott was convinced they would contain some clue to the whereabouts of the chemical weapon stash.

Eventually, one of the clocks in Bargemon struck midnight and he sat up, tossed aside the duvet and went over to the window. In the direction of La Maison were white flashes of light. He watched the display for a few minutes; fireflies always fascinated him. Then he looked more carefully. The flashes were too large for fireflies and they seemed to be following a regular pattern. As he continued to watch them, he became more and more suspicious of their origin. After a few minutes of careful observation, he got dressed, picked up a torch, checked the keys to La Maison were still in his trouser pocket and stole silently out of the house, skilfully avoiding the attention of the soldier posted in the grounds.

There was a bright moon in the clear night sky and the blue luminescence helped him to find his way. He crept into the hotel grounds and, as he did, the flashes stopped. Scott suspected it was some form of signal and as he moved closer to the building he heard a low droning noise. He listened to it warily for a moment, before instinctively sprinting to the side of the house. A few seconds later, a car with its lights extinguished entered the drive. Scott suddenly felt very vulnerable. He saw a crack in the wooden steps leading up to the front door of the house and made a run for it. It wasn't large, but he was just able to squeeze through the small niche into the space beneath the steps. The wood had shrunk and rotted slightly, which was fortunate, because the chinks in the structure gave him a limited view of the surrounding area. His heart was pounding wildly as the vehicle pulled up by the side of the steps and three people emerged from it. One of the occupants lit a cigarette and, for a brief moment, Scott could clearly see it was a woman. He looked at her face in the brief glow of the illuminated match. The angular bone structure of her face made her appearance very striking. Then the match was extinguished and the only light was from the moon and the pale red glow of the cigarette. They spoke quietly and although he couldn't make out the words, he was sure they were speaking in French. To his amazement, they went up the steps directly above him, unlocked the door, opened it and went inside. Scott was in a dilemma. Should he make his escape and risk them not coming back, or should he stay put? He felt confident that he was secure and his years of training as a soldier influenced his decision to remain hidden.

It was a long, uncomfortable wait. A plethora of unidentified nocturnal bugs scuttled over and around his body. Slightly unnerved by the creatures, he lay very still, hoping desperately that there weren't any scorpions and that he wouldn't be stung. He had to wait for over an hour before he heard the sound of movement again in the house. The two men came out, each carrying a box and for the first time Scott noticed a third man materialise from the vehicle. He held his breath, realising that they had a lookout, and blessed his good judgement for remaining concealed as the men took the boxes down the steps and loaded them into the back of the car. The woman locked the door and rejoined her accomplices. The car was restarted and they drove off into the still blackness of the night. He heard the car pull out of the gravel drive onto the road and then the sound rumbled off into the distance.

The wildlife chatted noisily around him and he deliberately remained hidden for nearly thirty minutes. When he was confident it was safe, he scrambled out from beneath the step, very stiff after his long, cramped confinement. There didn't seem any point in exploring the tunnel now, so he stretched and flexed his muscles, before silently making his way back to the villa. Arriving back at Pimaquet, he once again avoided the guard and stole quietly into his bedroom, his brain digesting all the events he had witnessed. He threw his shirt and trousers on the floor and once again lay wide awake on the bed.

Who the hell was that woman? Was that the consignment of biological weapons and why were they moving it tonight? I should have explored the tunnel thoroughly this afternoon and found it! Why did I wait? Now, I've probably missed the one opportunity to stop the shipment from being delivered to Britain. Should I contact the NCB and let them know what happened? No, I'll do it when it's light…

As he considered everything, Scott finally succumbed to exhaustion and before he knew it, had drifted into an uneasy sleep.

The air was coloured a hazy, murky blue as Ben walked out of the bathroom and went over to Carla. She was naked and waiting expectantly for him on the bed. Carla turned to face Ben and, as he came up to her, she gently stroked his flat, toned abdomen. Carla reached out for him, but she had changed. She looked like another woman. A familiar looking woman, with a cigarette in her mouth, but Scott (or was it Ben?) couldn't identify her. Ben bent down and kissed her, but abruptly she had now transformed back to Carla.

Scott looked around in panic. He was no longer in his room. He was back under the steps of La Maison. It was dark. Ben was above him, hacking away at Carla's body with a cleaver. He had never seen Ben look so manic. Ben hacked away remorselessly at her arms, then at her legs and finally her throat. He stopped and looked down at Scott, lying shaking in the recess below and smiled threateningly. Blood dripped down through the wooden slats and splattered Scott's body. All of a sudden, Ben was chopping away at the steps and pulling away the rotten wood with unnatural power. Scott was exposed. Carla's severed head fell onto his chest. He screamed, but there was no sound.

Before he could react, Ben was coming towards him. The blood-soaked cleaver was still in his hand. Closer and closer he came. The cleaver was held above his head ready to swipe down onto Scott's exposed body. Scott tried to call out again, but still there was no sound and Ben kept coming, closer and closer...

'No Ben!' he shouted. 'Ben, please get away from me! Ben!'

Ben's empty hand grabbed hold of his shoulder, the cleaver was raised above his head, ready to strike its horrid blow. Scott cried out again.

He suddenly came to. Carla was shaking him and he relaxed, realising at last that it had been a nightmare.

'Scott, whatever were you dreaming about?'

'Dreaming about? What do you mean?'

'You were shouting out Ben's name.'

Scott looked around. It was dark in his room and the dim illumination came from the light on the landing. 'What time is it?'

'It's just after three in the morning. Are you alright now?'

He sat up and started to tell Carla about his moonlight visit to La Maison. As he continued with his tale she watched him in bewilderment. When he had finished, she said: 'Scott, you must have dreamt all this. You're just like Ben with these nightmares!'

'No, it was all too real. I didn't dream it. I went to La Maison and I saw three people go in and collect some cases. It must have been the biological weapons.'

Carla shook her head. 'Scott, your visit to the hotel was a part of a nightmare. You didn't visit the house tonight, you didn't hide under the steps and you didn't see people go in and come back out again with boxes. It was no more real than Ben trying to attack you.'

Scott sat bolt up right in his bed and looked at her.

'I am not accustomed to imagining things! Why don't you believe me?'

'It's not that I don't believe you, but you have to admit Scott, your story doesn't sound very likely.'

He stared at her determinedly.

'I did see flashing lights and I did go to the house!'

He ran his hands through his hair. It was dirty and dusty and he could feel pieces of dried vegetation clinging to some of the hairs. He jumped up, went over to the light switch and turned it on. When the room was fully lit, he went over to a mirror and looked at himself.

'Look at me; I'm filthy dirty! Do you recall me being in this state before we went to bed tonight?'

He picked up his jeans and shirt, discarded in a heap on the floor.

'Look at these,' he demanded. His clothes were dusty and soiled, just as if he had been lying in a cramped and dirty cubby hole. 'This didn't happen in a dream!'

Carla stared at him.

'No, it didn't. You've certainly been somewhere.'

She stood up, looking first at his dirty body and then at the pile of clothes that Scott had thrown back onto the floor. He picked up his mobile phone and activated the flip.

'Who are you calling?' she asked.

'Monique. I think the three of us need to pay an early-morning visit to La Maison.'

When it was light, Carla went with Scott over to the hotel. As they met up with Monique, she was still thinking things through, confused and dreading her inevitable return to the cavern beneath La Maison. She hadn't been able to sleep after Scott's nightmare and had lain in bed, desperately trying to make sense of everything that had occurred. Was it possible that Scott visited La Maison, as he claimed, or had he been sleepwalking like his brother was prone to do? She was suddenly aware that he was speaking to her.

'I was here when I heard the car approaching,' said Scott, standing by the steps near the front door. 'I ran to the side of the house and hid under the step.'

They went over to the decking and inspected the wooden dais. It did appear that something, or someone, had recently forced its way underneath. Some of the wood had been ripped off and the space below suggested something had been lying there. Scott was triumphant.

'There, I told you it wasn't a dream! I was lying down there last night, exactly as I described it to you.'

'It's possible,' commented Carla, not sounding too convinced. 'It certainly looks as if something was there.'

Scott looked at his sister-in-law in exasperation, realising he still hadn't curtailed her scepticism.

'You still think I imagined it all, don't you?'

Carla didn't answer.

'Let's go inside and see if we can find anything,' she replied evasively.

Scott shot her a frustrated glance and went up the steps and unlocked the front door. In the hall nothing had changed from their visit the day before. They went over to the escape tunnel and activated the mechanism. When it was open, Scott went back to the front door, closed it and locked them in.

'What are you doing?' asked Monique, a little startled, as Scott pocketed the key.

'I'm just taking precautions. I realise that I still haven't convinced you both about what I saw last night. However, I don't want whoever it was coming back and finding the front door open.'

Scott took two torches from his pocket and, after giving one to Carla, he opened the entrance to the concealed passage. She hesitated, not wanting to return to the damp, unappealing void. On this occasion, she at least felt more prepared for the onerous ordeal, but was still very reluctant to return to the gloomy subterranean world beneath the hotel. When they were safely inside, Scott activated the closing mechanism. He placed a reassuring arm around Carla's shoulder and she anxiously looked behind her, alarmed as the solid barrier resealed them in the sinister claustrophobic tunnel. She suddenly panicked and desperately wanted to escape the repressive blackness. However, the desire to find out who had attacked Ben was stronger than she had first realised. She took a deep breath of the musty air, bravely swallowed her fear and followed Scott and Monique cautiously through the cold, damp interior, deep into the bowels of Provence.

As they moved down the steep, slippery path, the walls narrowed, closing them in and adding to her fear. Carla noticed as they continued with their journey that this genuine secret tunnel wasn't strewn with cobwebs, unlike the mythical passageways of her childhood literature. They arrived at the stone steps leading up to the church in Bargemon and the echo of their footsteps, accompanied by the droplets of water dripping from the domed ceiling, made mysterious hollow sounds. The walls of the tunnel continued to narrow noticeably and Carla felt once more as if she was being engulfed by the clammy darkness.

When they reached the steps leading up to the church in Callas, Monique and Carla stopped, but Scott continued to follow the line of the tunnel. The two women eventually followed him and were surprised to find him shining his torch all over the surface of the bricked-up dead end. He was deep in thought, recalling a previous experience in a similar tunnel, when Carla and Monique reached him.

'What are you looking at?' asked Monique. 'I told you yesterday that this part of the tunnel was blocked off years ago because it was structurally unsafe.'

'Yes, I do seem to recall you saying something about that. Do you know when it was done?'

'During the Second World War, I think, but I'm not absolutely sure.'

He was only half-listening to Monique as he looked carefully at the barricade blocking the remainder of the tunnel. He went over to it and they watched him in puzzlement as he fumbled around in a corner adjacent to obstruction. Eventually, Monique was unable to contain her curiosity.

'What are you doing, Scott?'

'If I'm right, there'll be an opening mechanism around here somewhere,' he answered, engrossed with groping the wall. 'Ah, yes, here it is.'

There was a barely audible click and the barrier slid slightly to the left, making a gap just large enough for an adult to squeeze through. They both stared at him in astonished admiration.

'There we are! I saw a couple of these hidden escape routes when I was working in Iraq last summer. I thought I recognised it yesterday afternoon, but everything finally came back to me a couple of minutes ago.'

They shone the torch through the entrance and could see an extension to the passage on the other side. Hanging from the ceiling were strands of cobweb, which now waved slightly in the barely-moving air. Her confidence beginning to return, Carla was about to enter the tunnel and brush the feathery gossamers aside, but Scott stopped her.

'Be careful, and don't touch those cobwebs!'

'Why not?'

'Didn't you notice that there weren't any cobwebs at all in the main tunnel?'

'Yes. And the point you're making is?'

'Doesn't it seem strange to you that suddenly in this concealed section of the tunnel there are cobwebs?'

'Not really.'

'They're markers to check that no one else has passed down here. So, be very careful not to knock into them!'

They squeezed carefully through the narrow opening and moved cautiously through the passage. Scott, alert at all times, carefully ensured they didn't disturb anything. After a few minutes, they could see tiny, intense shafts of light, permeating vibrantly from the surface. They came to the end of the tunnel and observed a rickety wooden ladder leading towards a wooden trapdoor – the source of the pinpricks of light. All around the base of the ladder, on the dusty ground, were prominent indentations – suggesting large objects had been lying there.

Scott looked first at the ground and then up towards the sur-face and announced: 'This must be one of the storage areas. There are probably a number of them built into the length of the main tunnel.'

He turned to Carla. 'I bet the boxes I saw last night were stored in here.'

Carla came up to him, the light from the surface affording her some comfort. She looked closely at the marks on the dusty floor. 'Yes, Scott. I think you're probably right.'

'So, you believe me now?'

'I'm sorry I doubted you.'

Scott didn't need to reply. He was content to know that Carla finally accepted his story. He turned his concentration back to the problem in hand. 'Monique, do you know how your parents stored and moved the consignments?'

'No, they were careful not to involve me in any of it.'

'They must have stockpiled everything in cubbyholes like this and then, when it was safe, used different exits to move it out.'

He shone his torch around the area, scrutinising everything. 'They had quite an efficient little set-up, didn't they? I wouldn't be surprised if the shipment we're tracking was down here on the night of the storm.'

'If it was here, why didn't they move it on the night Ben was attacked?' asked Carla, confused.

'These storage areas are very secure and I don't suppose many people even know of their existence. The police didn't find anything when they searched down here, did they...?'

Of course, Scott thought to himself. *Mauron must have ensured they didn't! O'Sullivan, you're an imbecile!*

'I imagine CAT thought it would be safer to move it later, when things had gradually died down,' Scott continued aloud.

Carla thought through the logistics of Scott's conclusions for a few seconds. 'Why did they decide to move it last night and then take it out through the front door? That seems a very stupid thing to do!'

Scott shook his head. 'We don't know what time plan they're working to; neither do we know what damage had been done to the surrounding area. It's possible that some of the other exit routes had been temporarily blocked or were inaccessible.'

'The surrounding land has been badly storm-damaged,' confirmed Monique.

'Then, with me moving in next door, they probably realised the danger and decided to store it somewhere else. So they moved it immediately. I wonder where?'

I'm an incompetent idiot, Scott thought to himself. *I should have looked yesterday!*

He turned back to Monique. 'Are you sure you didn't hear anything about when the consignment was due to be moved or where it was going?'

'No. My parents were very secretive about it.'

That's a shame, but I must continue to quiz you. I'm sure you know more than you're letting on.

Scott had a sudden thought, looked up at the hatch and moved towards the ladder. As he was climbing it, Carla asked: 'What are you doing, Scott?'

'I'm just wondering why they didn't use this exit point last night.'

He reached the top and attempted to open the cover at the top of the ladder. It wouldn't budge.

'It feels like there's something heavy lying on the hatch; maybe it's debris deposited from the storm.'

After several further unsuccessful attempts to open the trap-door, he gave up and descended the ladder.

'That explains why they took it through La Maison. Come on. I think we should get back to Pimaquet and discuss our next move.'

They made their return journey along the narrow passage, carefully negotiated the cobwebs and squeezed back in to the main tunnel at the entrance to Callas. Scott resealed the hidden entrance and they made their way back to the reception hall at La Maison. Once there, he closed the access in the house, unlocked the front door and let them out. Back in the bright morning sun, he checked the immediate area around the hotel. When he was quite confident that they weren't being observed, he led them quickly back to the house.

As they made their way along the mountain road back to Pimaquet, Monique asked: 'Scott, how did you know there would be a secret access beyond that bricked-up wall?'

'I didn't really. It was just a lucky guess. When I was in Iraq last summer, fighting insurgents, I was shown a number of fortifications with escape tunnels and storage areas like this one. They were built in kasbahs all over the Middle East during the crusades. When the Moors moved into Spain they brought the secret with them and built them into their fortifications. The technique proved so effective that it quickly spread across Central Europe.'

'So what made you think there might be one built into this escape tunnel?' asked Carla.

'It was a sudden burst of intuition. I was staring at that wall and my mind flashed back to my experience in the caves of Iraq. Suddenly I wanted to find the activation device.'

He was just finishing his sentence as they entered the kitchen of the house. They were taken aback to find Pierre sitting at the table, drinking a cup of coffee.

'*Bonjour, mes amis,*' said Pierre. 'I'm sorry to call on you at this early hour, but I just wanted to make sure that you were alright after your first night here.'

He looked over at Monique.

'I assume that you've all been to La Maison again.'

'Yes,' answered Scott, watching the policeman carefully.

'Did you discover anything of interest?'

'I'm afraid not. Have you made any progress?'

'Not really, but I do have some good news for you. Your brother has been responding very positively and the hospital think they may try and bring him round in a couple of days.'

'Oh, that's fantastic,' said Carla. She turned excitedly to Scott. 'I want to go to visit him later this morning!'

'That's a good idea. I have a couple of visits I want to make today, so we can do it after visiting the hospital.' He turned to Pierre. 'Inspector, Monique was telling me yesterday that there was a journalist with the team who had originally gone to airlift Ben out of La Maison. Apparently he's quite a local celebrity.'

'His name is Paul Barle,' answered Pierre. 'He's written a number of very controversial articles about alleged ritual killings in this area of France.'

'How did he get on board the helicopter?' asked Scott.

'I don't know, but we've instigated a disciplinary procedure against the officer in charge of the rescue operation and we've been forced to apply some pressure to curtail Barle.'

'Why? What's he saying?'

'He has some very strange theories about the murders and we can't possibly permit him to publish his ideas.'

'What does he think happened?'

'I really can't be bothered to go into any detail about his stupid ideas because it would be a complete waste of your time. The man has become obsessed with conspiracy theories at all sorts of levels in the community. He's convinced the killings were a form of sacrificial ritual. His speculations are complete nonsense and have no foundation to them whatsoever!'

'Is he freelance?'

'No. He works for *Le Monde* and is based in Nice, but I really would advise you not to waste your time.'

'It might be a waste of time, Inspector, but I would still like to discuss his theories with him.'

'If you really want to speak to him, ask to see Anton Condon at the offices in Nice. If you tell him that I gave you his name, you should find him very helpful.'

'Thank you, Inspector.'

'I really think you can call me Pierre; after all, we are supposed to be working together.'

'Maybe.'

Pierre finished his coffee and left them to organise the rest of their morning. After he had gone, Carla turned on Scott.

'You know, Scott, you really do need to treat Pierre a bit better than this. He offered you an olive branch then and you snubbed him.'

'He's a policeman, so I'm sure he will get over it!'

'Carla's right, Scott. Andre works in the same office as him and he says he is a really good police chief. He treats everybody equally, listens to all points of view and is a really nice man. You should give him a chance.'

'Let's see what Paul Barle has to say first, shall we? Can I suggest that I drop you off at the hospital, Carla, whilst I drive over to Nice and try and arrange a meeting with him? Then we could all meet up for lunch in Draguignan. How about the restaurant we ate in the night before last?'

'Can you drop me in Draguignan, too, please? I need to see my parents' *notaire* about the estate.'

Scott couldn't think of a reason not to comply with Monique's request, so he agreed.

With all the arrangements made, Scott drove the two women to Draguignan, reserved a table at the restaurant and then made his way along the coastal road to Nice. He entered the reception area of the *Le Monde* newspaper building confidently and told the receptionist that he had been sent by Pierre Mauron. His request for a meeting with the editor, Anton Condon, was accepted almost immediately. He listened considerately to Scott's request for an interview with Paul Barle and made a phone call to the journalist's office. Fortunately, he was at his desk and once again Scott didn't have to wait for very long before the journalist agreed to see him. Paul Barle also listened sympathetically to the reasons for Scott's visit, but confessed that it was unlikely that he could be of any assistance.

'You were one of the first people to arrive at the house when the bodies were found,' said Scott.

Paul Barle shuddered as he recalled the shocking images.

'I don't think that I will ever forget the shock as I wandered around. The killings were so horribly barbaric, particularly the woman in the kitchen. Her intestines were removed whilst she was still alive and they wrapped them around her neck.'

'Why do you think they did that?'

'I assume they wanted the authorities to know which group had carried out the executions, so they left a clearly recognisable symbol.'

Scott sat back, looking carefully at the journalist.

'It certainly could be something like that. Pierre Mauron told me that you have some very bizarre theories about the murders.'

'Pierre Mauron is an idiot!'

'Maybe, but the police don't seem to have an acceptable solution, so I would be very interested to hear your explanation.'

Now it was Paul Barle's turn to look warily at Scott.

'Monsieur O'Sullivan, have you ever studied the history of human sacrifices?'

'No.'

'Well, I have. I started to research it as a result of investigating the disturbing increase in ritualistic killings across Europe.'

'Is this leading anywhere?' asked Scott, slightly puzzled.

'Yes, I think so. During the last press conference, the police suggested the possibility of a religious cult breaking into the hotel and slaughtering everyone. There had been a few similar cases around here before. The police told me they believed they were linked to a local satanic sect.'

'Are you telling me that there have been similar murders to this in the past?' *Why the fuck didn't Mauron tell me this?*

'Yes and they've all involved the removal of the victims' intestines.'

Arsehole, Mauron! You should have told me, Scott thought to himself, before replying, 'You think it's some form of ritualistic killing, like a sacrifice?'

'Well, sort of, but I don't believe this is a result of the type of satanic group the police have in mind.'

'Why do you think that?'

'The pattern of the massacre, and the symbols they left behind, don't fit in with any of the ritualistic killings that I've ever studied.'

'So, what's your theory?'

'Do you know anything about freemasonry?'

'Not really, why?'

'When the brotherhood initiate a new member into the society, a rope is placed around the neck, called the cable-tow. The noose is supposed to symbolise the umbilical cord.'

'Are you suggesting that's why the intestines were wrapped around some of the victims' necks?'

'Yes, during one of the Masonic rituals, a piece of rope is removed from the neck to indicate it's no longer required by the user. It symbolises the cutting of an umbilical cord from a newborn baby.'

'And is carried out when they fall out of favour?' added Scott, still unsure of the course of Paul Barle's thoughts.

The journalist nodded. 'That's part of the process when a Mason is ejected from the brotherhood or disgraced.'

'Why do you think the La Maison killings and the other murders have a link with Masonry?'

'If you make an association with the pattern of symbols left at the scene of each crime, it's obvious.'

'Is it? But Monsieur Barle, why would Freemasons be involved in killing British tourists in a hotel in Provence?'

'Have you ever heard of Captain William Morgan?'

'No.'

'William Morgan was the first recorded victim of a Masonic execution. He claimed to have discovered the existence of a secret hierarchy close to the top of the Masonic structure, which he maintained endorsed devil worship. The group are known as "The Palladium". He published his findings and, as a result, became the first Masonic martyr.'

Scott stared at him, confused once again by the course of the discussion.

'What connection are you trying to make between this and La Maison?'

'They executed him by tying a rope around his neck and attaching weights to his legs. His intestines were ripped out and he was thrown into the Hudson River, where he drowned.'

'Are you trying to forge a link between this story and the murders at La Maison?' *You're a bloody crackpot!* thought Scott.

'It's not a story! This is historical fact and it caused such an outrage in America that Masonic membership dropped by over twenty per cent. There was a trial that lasted nearly three years, but it was all covered up. The real culprits, "those which remain unknown", were never questioned or prosecuted.'

'"Those which remain unknown"! Who the hell are they?'

'They are group of very powerful and influential Freemasons. Their identity is kept secret from all but a handful of the brotherhood.'

'Are you seriously trying to convince me that La Maison and the other killings are connected with some form of ritualistic Masonic execution?'

'I think it's possible, but I haven't been able to find the missing link to prove it. You see, all human sacrifices follow an identifiable pattern. The Aztecs, for example, cut open the chest cavity of the victim, ripped out the heart and then flayed the face with a pattern to represent the sun.'

Frigging loon! Scott thought to himself. 'Your links are very questionable, Monsieur Barle. The Aztecs were wiped out hundreds of years ago; how do you equate this with the attacks in the South of France?'

'I was just giving you an example of human sacrifices, but to answer your question, the Aztecs still practice their rituals, as do the Santeria.'

'What the bloody hell is the Santeria?'

'The Santeria developed as a kind of hybrid between ancient African religions and our own Roman Catholic Church. It gradually evolved into a practice called Voudon, better know in the West as Voodoo. Freemasons adopted many of the Santeria's rituals; in fact, all Masonic ceremonies can be traced back to the Santeria, including those concerning human sacrifice.'

'Don't be ridiculous! The Freemasons aren't pagan; they're a Christian organisation.'

Paul Barle laughed. 'You're quite mistaken, Monsieur O'Sullivan. It is definitely not a Christian organisation, quite the opposite, and the signs are all there, if you're prepared to interpret them properly.'

'What signs?'

'The intestines wrapped around the necks. Then there were the entrails arranged in the shape of a pyramid. What does that tell you?'

'It doesn't tell me anything.'

'Do you know how the Masonic hierarchy around the world is organised?'

'No.'

'It's a pyramid formation. The lodge members are at the bottom of the structure and a conclave of powerful and dangerous members are at the top. They've created a supreme hierarchy, a body of men that remain completely unknown to all other Masons. They're made up of the nine "Illuminati", the nine "Unknown", the "Seven" and ultimately "The Great Architect of the Universe" – often referred to as "The Lost Name". He's the order's most powerful leader, controlling the secrets at all Masonic levels. "The Great Architect of the Universe" hand-selects people to be initiated into "The Palladium". It's only then that they are instructed into the true meanings of the rituals.'

'And what is the true meaning of the rituals?'

'They aim to replace the Lord Almighty with the Fallen Angels, thus, establishing a "New World Order". That is their ultimate secret.'

Fuck me! Scott thought. *This guy's a fruitcake!*

'Mauron's right: you're off your rocker! This is a complete waste of my time,' he said aloud.

Paul Barle sat back, shaking his head in frustration.

'You aren't listening to me because you've been indoctrinated into thinking freemasonry is a caring organisation! I can assure you, Masonry is no such thing. It's a universal religion and senior Masons take a conscious decision to mislead and deceive those in the lower degrees. The true interpretation, the ultimate secret, is reserved only for "The Princes of Masonry".'

'I'm not listening to you because it's crap! Freemasons aren't antichrists. They're kind, caring people who do a great deal of good work for charities.'

'Well, that isn't what your own church says in England,' said Paul, going over to his filing cabinet. He took out a file, opened it, and showed Scott a document. 'This is from the minutes of the General Synod meeting in London, a few years ago.'

He read out a highlighted section of the minutes.

'"There are a number of very fundamental reasons to question the compatibility of Freemasons with Christianity",' he read. 'So, you see, even your own church agrees with me.'

'You haven't convinced me, Monsieur Barle.'

'The removal of the intestines from one of the victims at La Maison and arranging them in a pyramid formation is a direct indication of Masonic involvement. There is no doubt about it. I have researched this subject thoroughly.'

'I'm sorry to contradict you, but this is just garbage. How can you possibly link the structure of Masonry with the arrangement of the intestines at La Maison?'

'The Princes of Masonry use a diagram of human intestines arranged in the shape of a pyramid as their emblem. It's another of the secrets, known only to Esoteric Masons, and anyone who betrays the secrets of the brotherhood is severely punished.'

'This is ridiculous. My father's a Freemason. These people aren't religious fanatics!'

'It may all sound a bit far-fetched, but I have been researching this for years and it's the only explanation that fits in with the symbols that were left at La Maison.'

'Far-fetched! It's bloody ridiculous. I know one thing for sure: my brother was not attacked by fanatical Freemasons!'

Paul sighed.

'The pyramid of intestines, the rope taken from the victim's neck: it's all symbolic of Esoteric Masonry, a group that Mazzini describes as, "those who will remain unknown".'

'Who the fuck is Mazzini?'

'There's no need to swear, Monsieur O'Sullivan. Giuseppe Mazzini was a senior Italian Mason of the last century. He, along with Albert Pike, helped to establish the Esoteric tier of Masonry, a sect that they called "a supreme rite which will remain unknown".'

Scott shook his head in disbelief, but Paul Barle would not be deterred.

'They are never discussed or eluded to at any Masonic level below the Palladium, but they have complete control and influence over all aspects of Freemasonry.'

'Let's just accept for one moment that you are right, and I'm very doubtful about that. I'll ask you again. Why would a group of Freemasons be involved with the murder of all those people in a hotel in Provence?'

'I don't know,' Paul admitted. 'I can only assume that is was meant to be some type of warning to anyone who could read the signs.'

'I thought you said only a handful of people would be able to understand the signs.'

'Yes, I did, so it would have to be someone very powerful, one of "The Princes of Masonry", or even possibly the group above "The Palladium".'

'How do you account for the woman found dead in her bed? She wasn't marked at all.'

'It's interesting that you've picked up on that, too.'

'The police think she was dead before the attack commenced.'

'Even so, you would expect them to have left some type of mark on her. There must have been another reason why she was left alone.'

'What about my brother?'

'He was shot trying to escape, wasn't he? He fell in an awkward place; even the police had trouble getting to him. I think that's why he wasn't marked, but the woman in the bed puzzles me.'

'Have you told the police this?'

Paul laughed cynically.

'No. I haven't told an organisation, corrupted to the core by Freemasonry, that I suspect one of their brotherhood was responsible for the La Maison killings! Anyway, they won't let me say any of this in public.'

'Yes, well I am beginning to see why.'

Paul Barle sat back in his chair and sighed. He hadn't really expected Scott to understand.

'I'm sorry to have distressed and confused you. I can't get the memories of that terrible morning at La Maison out of my head, but I continually reach the same conclusion. Those people were killed, or sacrificed, for a definite reason. Discover the reason, interpret the symbols correctly and you'll find the assassins.'

Scott's head was spinning with confusion as he left Paul Barle's office and drove back for his luncheon rendezvous in Draguignan. CAT, Freemasons and Lost Names – it was all too incredible to contemplate. But he was gradually beginning to wonder if Paul Barle had been on the right track about interpreting the signs correctly. By the time he reached his destination, his scepticism had become significantly diluted.

At the restaurant, Carla and Monique listened to the account of his meeting with Paul Barle in amused disbelief.

'You had a wasted morning then,' said Carla, when he had finished his summary. 'Paul Barle is obviously completely mad!'

'He did raise some relevant points, especially about the need to interpret the signs correctly.'

'Did he?' asked Carla doubtfully. 'It all sounds like a lot of nonsense to me.'

'I'm afraid I have to agree with Carla,' admitted Monique. 'We know there was a plan to infiltrate the CAT group, but I really can't accept that Freemasons were involved.'

'Pierre was right; the man's obsessed!' said Carla.

'I was thinking about the meeting whilst driving back from Nice and I agree that it's unlikely to be linked to Freemasonry, but his theory about symbolism fits, doesn't it?'

'Only in the bizarre world of Paul Barle,' replied Carla. 'Ritual killings and pyramids of intestines; it's all rubbish! And to be honest, Scott, I'm surprised you're giving it any credence at all.'

'I think you're being too dismissive about some of his ideas. If we are going to solve this case, we need to look at everything with a more open mind.'

Carla shook her head and laughed.

'I'm sorry, Scott, but I really cannot accept that someone called The Great Architect of the Universe ordered the attack on Ben and I don't believe that you think that, either!'

They all laughed, including Scott.

'Come on, Scott. Finish your lunch and then we can go back to the hospital to visit Ben.'

'I was so wrapped up with reporting back the meeting with Barle that I completely forgot to ask after him. How is he?'

'He's responding positively to stimuli and they are very optimistic about his recovery.'

'Thank God. Well that's something to drink to!'

He took a sip from his glass of wine.

'Why don't you show Scott the picture I took on your phone of you and Ben the night before the storm?' suggested Monique suddenly.

Carla called up the picture gallery on her phone and selected one of them to view.

'Isn't that a nice photograph, Scott? When we get back to England, I think I'll download it and run it off.'

'You mean you actually want to have visual memories of that place?' asked Scott as he took hold of Carla's phone. He looked at it and was immediately distracted by the presence of a woman in the background.

'Who's that?' he asked, pointing towards the picture.

Carla looked at him curiously. His whole body language had suddenly changed. She checked the image that had caught Scott's attention.

'That's Sarah Radley. She's the woman who died from the sedative overdose. Why?'

Scott didn't appear to be listening. He was staring intently at the display on the phone, his mind flashing back and forth between the photograph on the screen and the memory of a woman with a cigarette in her mouth.

'Scott, whatever is the matter?' asked Carla, concerned.

Scott took a deep breath and looked slowly towards Carla.

'That's the woman I saw last night.'

The two women were silent for a moment.

'Don't be ridiculous,' said Carla, eventually. 'That's Sarah Radley. She died at La Maison.'

'I saw her last night!'

'How can you have seen her? She's dead,' said Carla decisively. 'I know she is a very striking woman, Scott, but you're mistaken.'

'Like I was with the dream?'

'That's different, and I have apologised to you about it, but this time you're wrong! Sarah Radley died the same night that Ben was attacked. You can't possibly have seen her.'

Scott glanced back at the mobile screen and then looked straight into Carla's eyes.

'That is the woman I saw lighting a cigarette.'

There was no doubting the integrity in Scott's dark, penetrating eyes. Not for the first time Carla felt as if she was conversing with Ben. She put her arm around his shoulder.

'Scott, think logically. You only saw her for a few seconds illuminated by a match. How can you possibly be so sure it was Sarah Radley?'

'As you said yourself, Carla, she is a very striking woman. She has the type of face you aren't likely to forget.'

Carla wasn't convinced. 'It was in the middle of the night, in very poor light, you were tired and had been drinking. Whoever you saw just resembled this woman; nothing more.'

'It was her, Carla! The woman in the background of this picture is the one I saw at the hotel last night.'

Carla looked at Monique in exasperation.

'Scott,' said Monique. 'Sarah Radley died from an overdose of sleeping tablets and she was buried yesterday.'

'Monique, we know she was part of an undercover operation to infiltrate a group of dangerous terrorists. We also know that they were killed, probably as Paul Barle suspects, to warn other members of the group not to betray them.'

'Hold on a minute,' interrupted Carla. 'The file we read yesterday clearly stated that she wasn't an undercover agent and had no knowledge of the operation. If you remember, she'd been told that her husband was investigating illegal immigration. So, she wasn't connected with this at all.'

'Nor was Susan Chapman, was she? Her husband had been seconded onto this from Customs and Excise, yet she was mutilated in the same way as the others.'

'But Sarah died before the attacks commenced,' Carla reminded him.

That's true, thought Scott. *So she must have been a CAT agent all along! Yes, this is making sense now.*

'Maybe something else occurred,' he said thoughtfully. 'Something we haven't considered yet.'

'Whatever do you mean?' demanded Carla.

'We're just making assumptions based on what we've read and been told.'

'Well, what else can we do?'

'We can consider other options. Maybe Paul Barle was right, all we have to do is interpret the signs correctly and the pieces of this jigsaw will slot together.'

'They're making an extremely distorted picture in my head,' answered Carla. 'The police think she committed suicide or accidentally overdosed on Restoril and alcohol, so what else could have happened?'

Scott didn't answer her question. 'That was Pierre Mauron's theory, I suppose?'

'Are you suggesting that Pierre is mixed up in all this?' asked Monique.

It's the only explanation to account for the failure of the police to uncover the hidden storage bay, he thought to himself, *and the reason behind all these leaks.*

'It's the only thing that fits at the moment,' Scott said aloud.

'So, how is this woman involved, then?'

'I'm not sure yet, but she was obviously working for CAT.' He put his hands to his head, desperately trying to clarify everything in his mind. 'I wonder what really happened at Les Baux.'

'Scott, you're losing the plot! I was there and I witnessed Colin Radley being blown off a cliff.'

'No you didn't. Nobody saw the accident and we only have Sarah Radley's version of what happened.'

An idea was forming in his head. 'I'm going to visit Les Baux tomorrow.'

'What do you think you'll find there?' asked Carla.

'The solution to this mystery, I hope. Will you come too?'

'Of course, but won't you tell us what you intend to do?'

'Oh, I just want to look around,' said Scott evasively. 'Can you come too, Monique?'

'Yes, but I really don't know what you expect to find there.'

'It's a long way. We will have to have an early start, so why don't you stay the night with us in Pimaquet?'

'OK. Andre is on night duty for the next few days so I could do with the company. Can we stop off at his apartment so I can pick up a few things?'

'Good,' said Scott and then quickly changed the subject. 'Now, if I'm right, we can expect Pierre to contact us very shortly, to inform us that he can't get clearance from the NCB to view the file.'

'Surely he would realise that would arouse our suspicions?' said Carla.

'Not necessarily. I think he doesn't realise that we suspect him of anything.'

They returned to Bargemon to organise the next part of their investigation. When they arrived at Pimaquet, there was a note from Pierre posted on the door.

'My friend,' it read in French. 'I called to see you again this afternoon, but unfortunately you weren't here. I have some bad news. Lyon won't release the file to me. I'll try again tomorrow and will let you know the result. I trust you are all well. Pierre.'

Scott watched them read the message with smug satisfaction.

'Perhaps we should ask him if he's a Freemason,' he said eventually, with a wicked glint in his eye.

Seven

It took just under three hours to complete the drive from Bargemon to Les Baux de Provence. They parked the car and walked into the bustling streets of the lower town, had lunch and made their way up the steeply-raked streets to the entrance of the ruined upper town. As they negotiated the narrow streets, packed with souvenir boutiques, Scott noticed something of interest and entered a shop to inspect it further. Carla and Monique followed him, only to find him admiring an enormous teddy bear with a bag of Herbes de Provence around its neck labelled *'Je t'aime Provence'*.

'Whatever are you doing with that?' asked Carla.

'I think I'll buy it for Ben. It might cheer him up when he is moved from ICU.'

'I shouldn't think he will want to be reminded that he's in a French hospital in Provence,' replied Carla mockingly.

'Well, it's sweet and it'll show him that his brother is really just a big softie after all!'

He was about to take it over to the cashier when Carla stopped him.

'Wouldn't it be a better idea to buy that on our way back down? You'll get very hot carrying that around the upper town.'

'They've only got one left and I don't want to risk them selling it before we get back.'

'Why don't you ask the cashier to look after it and pick it up when we leave?' asked Monique.

'It isn't a problem. I don't mind carrying it.'

Carla didn't bother to argue with him further, being well used to his eccentricities. He handed over his credit card and, once authorised, they left the shop with Scott carrying the large bear under his arm. They paid their entrance fee and moved onto the hot, windy plateau. The view across the valley was spectacular and they wandered around for almost an hour, admiring the amazing vistas. Scott had bought a number of guides on the area the day before and had spent much of the evening scanning and absorbing the information. He was therefore able to take them on a well-informed guided tour of the encampment, explaining the historical significance of each section of the ruined castle. Before they had left, he had logged onto the website of the local news paper *Bouches du Rhône Matin* and had studied the report of Colin Radley's death. As a result of this research, along with Carla's memory of the events, they were easily able to identify the section of the ruined town in which Colin Radley had died. It was a barren place, ravaged by centuries of bloody battles and wind erosion. They mingled with the other tourists and wandered around the exposed rocky plateau. They shuddered as they stood on the place where Colin had fallen. Carla noted that there was now a sign in place, warning visitors in several languages about the dangerous and sudden gusts of wind.

'They aren't risking another accident, I see,' she said cynically.

'No, but they still could do with putting in some more safety barriers!'

Carla looked at him. 'I assume we haven't come here to check up on Les Baux's health and safety regulations, so are you going to tell us why we're here?'

'I needed to try something out.'

'And have you found what you were looking for?'

'Yes, I think so.'

He looked up at the rock face that partially covered the small secluded area.

'I can see how no one saw Radley fall. The rock formation completely obscures this whole section and anyone looking down from the upper ruin wouldn't be able to see us standing here. It also reduces the visibility from the other end of the plateau quite considerably. She chose a perfect spot.'

'A perfect spot for what?'

'Never mind, Carla. Let's get back to the car.'

As they were walking away, Carla noticed that Scott was no longer carrying the bear, which he had insisted on buying for Ben.

'I wondered when someone would notice I wasn't carrying it.'

'Where is it?'

'I threw it over the edge of the cliff a few moments ago.'

'You did what? What the bloody hell did you do that for?'

'Now, now, mind your language!' he teased. 'Why I did it is irrelevant. What's important is that neither of you noticed.'

'What! Have you gone completely mad?'

Scott wasn't listening. He started approaching other tourists, asking if any of them had noticed him drop his bear over the edge of the cliff. Nobody had. After thoroughly questioning all the bemused tourists in the immediate proximity, he returned triumphantly to the two mystified women and declared: 'There, nobody else saw me do it either. What do you think of that?'

'I think you've joined Paul Barle in his world of madness!' answered Carla. 'Whatever is the point of all this?'

'Can't you see? The only person who saw Colin Radley fall off the cliff was his wife.'

'Yes, but we already knew that,' said Monique patiently.

'Look, you two, I've just tossed a very large teddy bear into the air and smacked it over the cliff with my fist. No one noticed me do it, including yourselves, and you were standing next to me!'

They all stared at him, finally beginning to understand the implications of his action.

'Now, just for one moment, let's imagine we've been transported back in time by a few days. Colin and his wife casually walk over to the edge of this cliff. Carla, you're over there with Ben and you turn round and see them, but the full view is impaired by that rock. You turn back to look at this eagle, which was circling around and suddenly there's a strong gust of wind. In all the confusion, whilst everyone was trying to keep their balance, she pushed him off the edge of the cliff. No one notices that there's anything wrong until she starts screaming. The police arrive, take statements and everyone agrees that the accident coincided with a gust of wind, although no one actually saw him fall. The police accept Sarah Radley's account and probably intend to interview her again. That meeting doesn't happen, because during the night she apparently overdosed on sleeping tablets.'

'Exactly! So you finally agree that she was dead, too,' said Monique.

Scott looked at them both with a deadpan expression and asked, 'Have either of you considered the possibility that she didn't actually die?'

Carla stared at him, not quite sure if he was being serious.

'Don't be ridiculous, Scott. We know she died!'

'How do we know, Carla?'

Carla looked at him, frustrated. 'Because we read it on an official file yesterday!'

'That could have easily been falsified. Is it possible that she was in some form of inanimate coma that was incorrectly diagnosed?'

'An inanimate coma? Do you mean like catalepsy?'

'Yes.'

'Are you seriously suggesting the woman was in some form of cataleptic coma?'

'It fits in with Paul Barle's speculations as to why she wasn't mutilated. It would also explain how I came to see her a few days later.'

'You saw someone who looked like her.'

'No, Carla. I saw Sarah Radley!'

'We're just going around in circles and not getting anywhere! Why can't you just accept that you were mistaken?'

'Have you forgotten about the teddy bear?'

'No, I haven't! You've demonstrated that it's possible to do something drastic here without anyone noticing, but it isn't proof that Sarah Radley pushed her husband off the cliff, or that the hospital produced a false death certificate. This is just too over the top for words!'

'In my business, this is quite tame,' replied Scott, ruefully.

'Scott, I agree with Carla. The whole thing does seem very unlikely.'

'It's more than unlikely,' interrupted Carla. 'It just couldn't happen! She was interred in Draguignan yesterday, wasn't she? We all know how meticulous the French authorities are. There's no way that she could have been accidentally buried alive!'

'She obviously had an accomplice,' said Scott, becoming irritated. 'Pierre could easily have arranged a false death certificate.'

'He couldn't sign it, however,' Monique pointed out. 'Only the pathologist would have been able to do that and wouldn't it have to be checked by the coroner?'

'This is all beginning to make sense now,' said Scott, not really listening to Monique.

He was about to continue but was checked by Carla.

'Nothing makes any sense at all! Let's say, for the sake of argument, that what you claim is correct and this woman was working for CAT. It doesn't explain how she was able to dupe the authorities, including doctors, into believing she had died. Do you know anything about catalepsy?'

'Yes, I wrote a dissertation on it at university.'

'Then you'll know that the patient doesn't stop breathing, so how could she have been mistaken for being dead?'

'Pierre coordinated the investigation – maybe he persuaded the pathologist to sign the death certificate.'

'No, I can't believe that, and we're back to Pierre again! Monique has already told you that he's highly regarded by his fellow officers. Why are you so obsessed with him being the enemy?'

'As I keep telling you, his body language isn't right.'

Carla looked over to Monique and they both shook their heads in disbelief. 'Scott, I really cannot believe that Pierre organised for Sarah Radley to kill her husband and then arranged a fake suicide. Can you, Monique?'

'No.'

'Nor can I believe that he was able to persuade a pathologist to sign a death certificate, without thoroughly examining the body. It's ridiculous and just couldn't happen!'

'Unless of course, they're both involved. I hadn't considered that.'

Carla sighed and tapped her chin, desperately trying to make sense of the confusion inside her head. 'Scott, I'm going to be straight with you. I don't believe you saw Sarah Radley at La Maison yesterday and neither does Monique. We think you saw someone who resembled her. I can see that we won't be able to convince you otherwise and I suppose it would be wasting our breath to suggest you consult with Pierre. So, I recommend that we visit the police pathologist tomorrow morning and put your theories to him.'

They drove back to Bargemon arguing all the way over Scott's allegations. When they arrived at Pimaquet, Scott showered and went to sit by the pool alone. He needed to think over everything, undisturbed. Scott knew that he had seen Sarah Radley at the hotel, but could also appreciate Carla's scepticism. Their visit to Les Baux had finally convinced him that she had murdered her husband and then skilfully avoided the later attack on the remaining agents. He was also certain that Pierre knew more than he was disclosing. His suspicions had been corroborated when he discovered that Pierre had failed to inform him about alleged copycat killings. Scott couldn't understand why Pierre hadn't told him about the other murders. Did this mean that he was working with CAT and could it be that he was Foxicat? Considering all the possibilities suddenly persuaded him to consult with someone at the NCB, so he went inside and connected his mobile to the Internet. He quickly logged onto the military site and activated the messenger program.

> I need to speak to someone about operation CAT at La Maison August 2005. 5903.

The reply wasn't long in coming and Scott typed a message explaining everything he had discovered and suspected.

> Can you verify Mauron?

The response was rapid.

> MAURON IS NOT AN ISSUE. DO YOU BELIEVE THE CONSIGNMENT YOU WITNESSED BEING MOVED WAS THE CHEMICAL WEAPONS?

Yes.

Is it still in Var?

I don't know. I think it's likely.

Trace and locate that consignment. The PM is beginning to get jumpy, so it needs to be located quickly.

Bloody politicians, he thought.

What about Foxicat?

Forget Foxicat for the moment and forget Mauron. FIND & HALT THAT CONSIGNMENT.

He sat back and considered his options before replying:

I'll need backup.

An agent will contact you tomorrow. The code phrase has been changed to 5E.

Scott looked thoughtfully at the screen. There was some information he needed.

I'm visiting the pathologist tomorrow to ask some questions. I need access to the Radley autopsy notes.

Which one?

Both.

The codes will be sent to your mobile. Be careful 5903: Broqua hasn't been cleared yet.

Is he a suspect?

He's under investigation but we have no information on him.

So it's like Mauron?

I HAVE NO COMMENT ABOUT MAURON, BUT DEAL WITH BROQUA CAUTIOUSLY.

Do you have anything on Monique Ribert?

SHE'S UNDER INVESTIGATION.

By her boyfriend?

YES. WHY DO YOU ASK? ARE YOU INVOLVED WITH HER?

Not yet!

I SEE YOU HAVEN'T CHANGED, 5903. IF YOU DO GET INVOLVED WITH HER THEN INTERROGATE HER DISCREETLY AND SEND US THE RESULT.

Is she suspected?

FRANCE THINKS SHE'S UP TO HER NECK IN IT. WE'RE SENDING THE CODES NOW. CONTACT US IF YOU NEED MORE.

Scott logged off the message board as his mobile bleeped with the access codes. He turned, aware of movement behind him. It was Monique.

'What are you doing, Scott?'

That's just what I was going to ask you, he thought to himself. 'I'm just trying to access the autopsy reports on Sarah and Colin Radley.'

'Why's your phone connected to the computer?'

'It blocks snoopers.'

'Can you speak to your bosses through it?'

Suddenly Monique's questions were taking on a sinister significance and ringing alarm bells in Scott's head. *Now why do you want to know that? What are you up to?* he thought.

'No, it just prevents me from being traced. Do you know the name of the police pathologist by any chance, Monique?'

'He was a good friend of my father's.' She looked away sadly.

'Was he now?'

'His name is Jean-Jacques Broqua. He and his wife often came over to us for meals. Why?'

Did he? Scott thought. *That's interesting.* 'I just wondered,' he replied aloud.

She put her hand gently on Scott's shoulder.

'Scott, you're a very attractive man.'

He looked up, momentarily.

'Yes, I know!'

Monique laughed and began gently caressing his shoulder with the tip of her fingers. It tickled and, as he tensed, she began to slowly move her hand down towards his chest. Scott was having none of it and quickly caught hold of her hand and moved it firmly away from his body. He looked over to her again and said: 'Monique, I have a great deal to do, so can you go and get me a glass of wine?'

Do you think you can seduce me? I'm far too good for that, thought Scott.

Monique looked slightly embarrassed and left the room to pour Scott a drink. When she had gone, he turned back to the VDU and opened the autopsy file on Sarah Radley. He read it through carefully. Each revelation filled his mind with new questions and problems, but they didn't provide any solutions.

She was French! he thought as he read the details on the file *That's a surprise and Carla didn't mention that she had a French accent.* She was brought up in the Middle East, married an Englishman just under two years ago and then obtained British citizenship. *Hmm, that would fit if she was working for CAT. Why was she buried in Draguignan then? Oh, I see, her parents were from here. Now, what killed her?* Acute sleep apnoea – *what the fuck does that mean?* – due to excessive alcohol levels in her blood. *BAL 0.40? Shit, how could she have drunk all that?* There were six hundred milligrams of benzodiazepine in her body. *Bloody hell! Six hundred milligrams! That sounds an awful lot! Is it possible to have taken such a large dose?* Scott's mind was working in overtime as he started piecing the information together.

'Carla, can you come here a moment?' he called out.

Carla came quickly, recognising the urgency in his voice.

'What is it, Ben? Oh, sorry, I mean Scott.'

Scott looked up and laughed.

'Oh no, Carla. You're not trying to seduce me too, are you?'

Carla laughed.

'No, Scott. Monique just told me about that little incident in here just now. You can't blame the girl; she's feeling very vulnerable at the moment and you are a very good looking guy.'

'Yes, I know.'

'And an arrogant shithead, too. Just like your brother! Now what do you want?'

'I've just been reading the autopsy notes on Sarah Radley. Her blood alcohol level was zero point four.'

'Zero point four? Are you sure that's right?'

'Yes, look.'

He pointed to some figures on the screen. Carla read them and said: 'You know what that means don't you?'

'Yes, forty per cent of her blood was made up of alcohol. What the fuck could she have been drinking?'

'God only knows! It must have been aviation fuel! Isn't there a chemical analysis on the report?'

Scott looked but couldn't find one. 'What's acute sleep apnoea?'

Carla smiled. 'It means she stopped breathing.'

'How could that happen?'

'Alcohol increases the toxicity of all the benzodiazepines, causing a drastic reduction in blood pressure and respiration. In extreme cases, the patient stops breathing.'

Scott listened carefully, taking in all the information. He turned his attention to the sedative levels.

'It also says that she ingested six hundred milligrams of Restoril. Is that possible?'

'Six hundred milligrams! Surely not? The maximum dosage is thirty.' She did a quick calculation. 'That would be twenty tablets.'

'Did the hospital give her that much?'

'No. She had one strip of ten doses; each at thirty milligrams.'

'Are you sure?'

'I checked the quantity before we left the hospital.' She thought for a few seconds before asking, 'Did she suffer from depression?'

'I don't know, why?'

'Temazepam is occasionally prescribed to treat anxiety and depression, but it's quite unusual.'

'There's nothing about that on this report.'

'Can you check it out?'

'Yes, but that will mean getting access codes to her private medical records.'

Carla stepped back from the computer screen for a moment, carefully considering everything she had just read.

'If that report's correct, then she must have deliberately overdosed.'

'But she can't have OD'd, because I saw her!'

'You can't have. Look at the bloody report!'

'It must have been fabricated.'

'Scott, pull yourself together! You know as well as I do that you can't fabricate an autopsy. There has to be more than one person present, and there are usually many more!'

'They've been planning this for ages. They could easily have arranged for everyone at the autopsy to be members of CAT.'

Carla put her head in her hands. 'Scott, you've obviously been working for too long in the Third World. This is France, in 2005. An autopsy is always videotaped; how could they have made that up!'

Scott laughed. 'That would have been simplicity itself. These people have unlimited resources and have you never heard of CGI?'

'What?'

'All you'd have to do is tape any old body being cut open and then enhance it with computerised images. They could have knocked that up in less than an hour.'

'I'm sorry, but this is ridiculous and I don't believe it could, or did, happen.'

'Carla, if you remember, NASA managed to fool the whole world into thinking they were watching live pictures of a man landing on the moon! The technology since that fraud has escalated to unbelievable levels of sophistication. I can assure you, if we ask to see a recording of the autopsy, it will be there and look authentic!'

Carla sighed in frustration. 'Alright, just for the sake of argument let's say that the autopsy was fabricated and they created a lavish computer enhanced video of someone made up to look like Sarah Radley. If they had gone to such ridiculous lengths to produce all this, why would they risk raising suspicion by citing such a large quantity of drug?'

'I don't know. How much would be fatal?'

'One hundred milligrams would have killed her, and that's without the alcohol.'

'So, how do we account for the additional three hundred milligrams?'

'We can't. She was definitely only given one strip of ten tablets and I thought that was too much. The stuff's very habit-forming.'

Scott was about to reply, but stopped as Monique returned with his glass of wine. He took a sip from the glass and then accessed Colin Radley's file. It added nothing more to what he already knew.

After they had all gone to bed, Scott crept downstairs to the computer and applied for a new set of codes. Once obtained, he diligently read Sarah Radley's medical records. They confirmed his suspicions. When he had memorised all the necessary information he shut down the computer and stole silently up the stairs to discuss some anomalies with Carla. She was fast asleep when he entered her room. In order not to disturb Monique in the next room, he crept over to his sister-in-law and quickly grabbed hold of her, clamping his hand firmly over her mouth to prevent her crying out. She woke up terrified and then relaxed when she saw it was Scott. He put his finger over her mouth to warn her to make as little noise as possible and when he was sure she wouldn't cry out, he released her from his grip.

Carla looked at him, shaken. 'What the bloody hell are you doing?'

'I don't want Monique to hear us.'

She relaxed further. 'Why not?'

He sat on the edge of the bed, allowing her to sit up comfortably and switch on the bedside lamp.

'My contacts think she might be working for CAT. That's why I didn't say anything about Radley's medical records earlier. I've just checked them out and the only medication she's been prescribed in the last five years is amoxycillin and chlorphenamine.'

'So, she wasn't taking any anti-depressants or sleeping tablets?'

'No. What would the chlorphenamine be for?'

'Hay fever, I should think.'

'Can you buy temazepam over the counter?'

'No, it's a class-three drug. It's illegal to be in possession of it without a prescription.'

'So where did she get the additional dosage from?'

'I've been thinking about this, Scott. She didn't even have access to the strip the hospital prescribed. When we arrived back from St Remy I gave them to Maria Ribert for safe keeping.'

'Why did you do that?'

'Her husband had just been killed, so we didn't want to give her an opportunity to harm herself!'

'Why didn't you hold on to them? Surely you were the best qualified?'

'Scott, I was on my honeymoon with your brother. I had no intention of spending my time administering sedatives to a suicidal widow!'

He grinned. 'No, I suppose not. What about the alcohol; where would she have got all that from?'

'They probably did the same as Ben and myself and bought it in a hypermarket on the way down here.'

'So, she can't have OD'd on the sedatives. Where would they have been stored and could she have accessed them herself?'

'I'm pretty sure Maria Ribert locked them in the hotel safe, but I'm not a hundred per cent certain. But, Scott, that stuff disorientates you – she wouldn't have been able to go downstairs and open the safe! Anyway, there was only three hundred milligrams in the pack.'

'How much did they give her at the hospital?'

'I don't know. It was done intravenously, but they wouldn't have risked exceeding the maximum dosage and, even if they did, the most they would have given her was forty milligrams and that wouldn't have been safe.'

Scott assimilated everything thoroughly before coming to his conclusion. 'So, there are only two possible outcomes: either she was murdered or the autopsy report is wrong.'

Carla looked at him despairingly.

'The autopsy report cannot be wrong!'

'But it was! It suggested that she died before the attack, but she can't have, because she didn't have that amount of sedative!'

Carla thought for a few seconds before answering. 'That's true, so obviously she was murdered.'

'No, that can't be right either. I've checked up on Paul Barle's claim and there have been murders with a similar pattern to the ones at La Maison. If it was carried out by the same group and that's likely, why did they perform such a bizarre group of executions on everyone else and poison Sarah Radley? It doesn't fit in with the other attacks.'

'Well, Ben was just shot, wasn't he?'

'I don't think they meant to harm Ben. I suspect they intended him to find the bodies the next day. Anyway, Paul Barle told me that he had fallen in a place which was very difficult to access.'

'I wouldn't take any notice of anything that Paul Barle says. He's completely mad and, to be honest Scott, after listening to theories about digitally enhanced autopsy videos, I'm beginning to wonder about your sanity, too!'

Scott laughed. 'I realise it all sounds over the top to you, but I'm not very often wrong.'

'I know, and that's what's frightening the crap out of me! So, what are we going to do?'

'I think we need to see what the pathologist says tomorrow.'

'Are we taking Monique with us?'

'No. We need to put her off somehow. Perhaps we can say that it might be too much for the hospital if all three of us visited the pathology department and suggest that she stays here and prepares some lunch for us all. It's a bit sexist, but it's the best thing I can think of at the moment.'

Carla smiled.

'That should work, especially if we can convince her that we're combining the trip with visiting Ben, too.'

'OK, Carla, you can tell her in the morning because I think she still trusts you. Now, we need to get some sleep. We have a lot to do tomorrow.'

After he had gone, Carla lay in bed considering everything she had learned. Somehow, she had to convince Scott that he was mistaken. It was obvious that Sarah Radley had been murdered along with all the other victims. Scott's theory of forged autopsies and catalepsy was just too preposterous to even contemplate. She also knew that Sarah didn't have access to six hundred milligrams of sedative, so suicide was beginning to look less likely too. The only possible explanation was that an additional dose had been injected into her blood stream whilst she was unconscious. Hopefully, their meeting with the pathologist in the morning would persuade Scott that his conclusion was absurd.

Carla was exhausted and closed her eyes. Gradually, her thoughts began to blur and she drifted into an uneasy sleep.

Eight

When it was light, Scott drove to Draguignan with Carla. Having persuaded Monique to stay at Pimaquet, they were able to speak openly together, without fear of being overheard.

'Scott, I've been thinking about what you said last night. If Monique is involved, why is she so anxious to cooperate with us?'

'CAT must be paying her to keep an eye on what we are doing.'

'Surely not? She seems so genuine.'

'She would have to be, wouldn't she? We're not dealing with amateurs, Carla.'

'What about the pathologist? Can we trust him?'

'I don't know. He's not been cleared yet.'

'So why are we risking speaking to him?'

'There are several issues I need to clarify and hopefully he'll provide some of the answers.'

'Do you think the chemical weapons are still in Var?'

'Yes, and so does the British NCB. They must have decided to move the weapons after confirming my identity at Pimaquet, but time's running out and they can't afford to hold onto them for much longer.'

'So what are you going to say to Dr Broqua?'

'I'm going to tell him about the classified file and monitor his reaction.'

'Is that wise, Scott?'

'Probably not, but it'll be a good test for him.'

'Are you going to tell him about Sarah Radley?'

'I don't know. It's probably best to play everything by ear. You can be sure of one thing, though Carla: if he is working for CAT, I'll flush him out!'

On arrival at the hospital, they went straight to the pathology labs and were surprised to be granted an interview almost immediately. Jean-Jacques Broqua's genuine concern for their welfare enabled Scott to quickly reveal the existence of the classified file without rousing the pathologist's suspicions. He convincingly used the ruse of consulting a friend in the army to explain how he had gained access to the confidential dossier. Dr Broqua accepted Scott's explanation and listened intently, appearing to be appalled, as they revealed the true identity of the guests.

'I suspected there was something strange going on in that house. The killings were so brutal that it doesn't surprise me it was linked with smuggling and terrorism.'

He sat back and looked at them carefully. 'I don't really understand why you've come to see me, though. Surely, you should be speaking to Pierre Mauron?'

Carla and Scott looked uneasily at each other. Scott spoke first.

'The truth is, Dr Broqua, we don't trust Inspector Mauron. We suspect that he might have links with Foxicat, so we came to you to ask advice.'

He watched them cautiously, his face betraying nothing, before asking: 'Have you spoken to anyone else about this?'

'No, before we notified anyone, we wanted to hear what you had to say.'

'That's probably wise but are you quite sure that you've told me everything?'

Carla and Scott exchanged glances again and Jean-Jacques Broqua was quick to pick up on their indecision.

'You need to tell me everything you know, and also explain to me why you think I can help you.'

Scott decided it was time to test the pathologist further.

'You're right, of course. I have a theory that one of the victims in the hotel wasn't really dead. I saw her at La Maison, a couple of nights ago.'

Jean-Jacques looked quite taken aback.

'At La Maison a couple of nights ago! Impossible!'

Scott told him what he had seen when he visited La Maison in the middle of the night and explained about the picture on Carla's mobile phone. The pathologist was horrified.

'Are you telling me that you went to the house on your own, knowing full well it was being used by dangerous terrorists? Monsieur O'Sullivan, that was very foolish of you.'

'Yes, it probably was, but at the time I didn't consider myself to be at any risk.'

The pathologist studied him carefully. 'Well, perhaps you should have done!'

Scott looked at him. *Did I detect a threat behind your veiled reply, Dr Broqua?*

'Maybe,' he answered dismissively and then quickly changed the subject.

'Dr Broqua, in your professional judgement is there any possibility that any of those people, apart from my brother, were still alive?'

Jean-Jacques Broqua stared at Scott, obviously shocked.

'Are you seriously claiming that you saw Madame Radley two nights ago?'

'Yes, Dr Broqua.'

The pathologist looked at Carla, who just shrugged her shoulders. He sighed and sat back in his chair.

'It's not possible! I personally examined all the bodies of the victims and none of them were alive. Apart from your brother, they had either been shot through the head or mutilated.'

Hmm, so it was you! Let's try pushing this a bit further shall we? thought Scott. 'Sarah Radley's body wasn't violated though, was it?' he asked.

'No, but she had taken a massive overdose of a benzodiazepine.'

Scott desperately hoped Carla wouldn't give him away as he asked: 'What was the drug level found in her blood?'

Carla didn't react in any way as the pathologist answered: 'I can't remember the exact figure, but it was enough to kill her. I could look it up for you.'

Six hundred milligrams isn't a quantity you would easily forget! thought Scott.

'That would be very good of you Dr Broqua, but is it possible that she was in a cataleptic coma? In that condition, don't the limbs become stiff and the metabolic rate slow right down?'

Jean-Jacques looked startled. 'Catalepsy is a form of epilepsy, Monsieur O'Sullivan. In its extreme form the patient enters a trance-like state, with a loss of voluntary motion. If she'd been cataleptic, it would have been recorded on the central database. That would have been validated when the death was registered.'

I've obviously taken you completely by surprise! Scott thought to himself. *Why are you giving us a lecture about catalepsy and not telling me to fuck off?*

'Not necessarily, Dr Broqua,' he said aloud. 'It would only have been cross-referenced if there had been any doubt about the cause of death.'

'I have to tell you that I'm not comfortable with this conversation!' he confessed. 'During a cataleptic fit, the heart doesn't stop beating and the patient is still breathing. When I examined the body, her heart had stopped and she wasn't breathing.'

'Are you absolutely sure?'

Dr Broqua shook his head in irritation and sat forward. Momentarily, Scott thought that he detected a tiny bead of sweat materialising on the pathologist's brow. 'Of course I'm sure! I wrote that death certificate and I can assure you, Monsieur O'Sullivan, she was dead!'

Well, one of us is mistaken and it's not me! So, you must be an important part of CAT's scheme, he thought to himself before asking: 'Is there any possibility that one of the hospital staff made an administrative error?'

'No, I've already told you. I recorded all the details myself.'

I just wanted to make sure, Dr Broqua. After all, we don't want to arrest the wrong people!

The pathologist sat back and looked carefully at Scott. 'If you're able to come back tomorrow, I'll bring out my files and we can go through them. If, by some chance, there is an anomaly, it will be in my notes.'

Why can't we do it now? thought Scott.

'Thank you,' he said. 'We're very grateful for your support.'

Dr Broqua looked at Scott sympathetically. 'You'll be wasting your time, though. The woman was dead.'

'And I know that I saw her!'

'You're a very persistent young man. Come back tomorrow at ten o'clock and we'll go through the autopsy report. It might be advisable, though, if you didn't speak to anyone else about this for the moment.'

They didn't see him watching them carefully as they made their way out of his office. When he was sure they had gone, he reached for his phone.

Scott and Carla argued heatedly as they made their way through the hospital to ICU.

'Dr Broqua examined Sarah Radley's body personally and concluded that she was dead.'

'Carla, he's lying. The guy's up to his eyeballs in all this!'

'You're very quick to apportion blame on to people. Why can't you just accept that you were mistaken?'

He stopped and caught hold of her arm. 'Why do you think he lectured us about cataleptic fits? Wouldn't it have been more convincing if he had told me not to be so bloody ridiculous?'

'Yes, I wondered why he didn't do that.'

'He didn't because he knew that woman was in a cataleptic coma and we took him off guard!'

'So, what are you going to do now?'

'I need to speak to Pierre Mauron and insist that he exhumes the body.'

'But what if they are both working with CAT?'

'Well, this should bring one, or both of them, out into the open.' He paused, considering all options precisely. 'After checking on Ben, we need to go back to Pimaquet and pick up Monique.'

'Why? You said she was a suspect.'

'I think my contacts might be wrong about her and I'm suddenly feeling concerned for her safety.'

'Alright Scott. I'll go along with whatever you say, but wouldn't it be better for me to drive over to Bargemon after we've seen Ben? I could quickly pick her up and meet you at the police station?'

'OK. We mustn't give them the opportunity to reorganise, so it's probably better to go along with your idea. I can keep Mauron occupied whilst you collect Monique.'

'What about Dr Broqua?'

'We'll just have to hope that he hasn't had the time to contact anyone, but I should think he'll wait until after the meeting tomorrow morning before taking any action. Come on, let's go and see how Ben is.'

They arrived at ICU and were updated on Ben's progress. Dr Krasniqi was very pleased with his responses to stimuli, the IPL had returned to within the normal range and he was considering bringing him out of the induced coma in the morning. They left the hospital with mixed feelings, optimistic about Ben, but dampened by the conclusions they had reached after their visit to the pathologist.

Scott drove over to the police station and they swapped places. He'd already contacted Monique by mobile phone.

'We won't have much time after I've spoken to Mauron, so come straight back. We should be safe here and if necessary I can make direct contact with the General Secretariat in Lyon.'

He opened the glove compartment and took out his gun.

'Keep that close by you, just in case.'

'I don't know how to use it!'

Scott quickly demonstrated.

'Make sure your phone is on. I'm on speed dial, aren't I?

'Yes,' she replied, checking her mobile. 'Oh no, Scott, I've only got one bar left on the battery!'

'Have you got Ben's phone?'

'Yes, it's in my bag. Why?'

'We can't risk your phone discharging, so make sure Ben's is turned on. I know he'd charged it up just before the attack. If we need to contact each other quickly then we can use the speed dial. I think I'm number three on his. Try it.'

Carla activated Ben's phone and after it had initialised she pressed and held key number three. In less than thirty seconds, Scott's mobile rang with Ben's name illuminated on the caller ID.

'There's one more thing: put Monique's mobile number into Ben's phone.'

Scott read out the number and Carla saved it in the address book.

'I think we've taken all the necessary precautions. Pick up

Monique and I'll see if I can organise an audience with Inspector Mauron.'

Scott watched Carla drive off and then headed into the police building. He made his request to meet with Pierre and was shown straight into his office. Pierre was at his desk and appeared to be waiting for him.

'Where's Carla?'

'She's gone back to the hospital to sit with my brother? Why?'

'No particular reason.'

Pierre suddenly sounded very sinister. 'When did you first suspect that I was Foxicat?' he asked.

'From the moment I first met you.'

Pierre didn't answer. He reached into his drawer and pulled out a gun.

'Now, we must talk.'

He put the gun down on his desk.

As Carla approached Pimaquet, she was beginning to wish she hadn't suggested collecting Monique and instead, had accompanied Scott to the police headquarters in Draguignan. Turning into the drive, there was an inexplicable and painful acidic tightness in her stomach. She didn't know what had brought on the sudden pangs of anxiety, but it wasn't curtailed when she noticed that the police guard didn't appear to be on duty. Pulling up by the side of the house, she was surprised to discover that Monique wasn't waiting outside for her. Her phone had discharged as she reached Callas and she had rung from Ben's mobile, telling Monique she would be with her in a few minutes. Monique had assured her that she would be ready and it was disconcerting to discover on arrival that she wasn't anywhere in sight. In order not to cause any alarm, she hadn't told Monique the reason for the sudden change of plan, but she still had expected her to be ready. Carla suddenly felt comforted by the presence of Scott's revolver and she picked it up, placing it in her pocket along with Ben's mobile phone. Walking away from the car, she noticed how quiet the surrounding grounds appeared to be and, inexplicably, there was no sign of either the police or Monique.

She stopped in her tracks, instinct warning her that something wasn't right. Looking around, there wasn't anything out of the ordinary, but the painful cramp in her stomach wasn't abating. Before she knew what she was doing, she had taken hold of Ben's mobile phone and pressed speed dial number three.

Don't be ridiculous, Carla, you silly cow! she thought as the phone started to connect and immediately pressed the cancel key. *There's nothing wrong here! Now, sort yourself out woman! Whatever would Ben and Scott think?*

She continued to listen carefully but, other than the persistent sound of wildlife, everything remained disturbingly quiet. Taking a few steps forward, she suddenly heard the sound of a snapping twig behind her. Startled – and as a precaution – she took a firm grasp of Scott's revolver, ensuring it was ready to fire. Her skin burst into a cold sweat and her heart was pounding loudly as she began to move slowly in the direction of the sound. She started to tremble uncontrollably, realising there was something in the shrubbery and it was coming towards her. Her flesh began to crawl and she raised the revolver in the direction of the cracking twigs and crunching dry undergrowth. The damp sticky finger on the cold trigger was ready to fire the revolver and for one horrible moment, she thought her legs would give way. She was shaking with fear but somehow managed to hold the gun steady and aimed it determinedly towards the bushes. Suddenly her heart felt like it had missed a beat and she just stopped herself from pulling the trigger as the cat that had frequented the grounds during their stay rushed out of the undergrowth and trotted over to her. Carla sighed with relief and began to regain control of her laboured breathing. The animal rubbed affectionately around her legs, meowing loudly, hoping for a saucer of milk, which Carla had provided on a couple of occasions. She stroked the cat gently and tickled his ears.

God, this is ridiculous! she thought to herself.

'You silly boy, you made me jump! Do you want some milk?'

The cat looked up at her, purring expectantly, and Carla smiled at the vacant expression, which reminded her of how she always felt when people were conversing fluently in French around her.

'I suppose you haven't got a clue what I'm saying, have you?'

She stroked the cat again and then realised he was rubbing

around and attempting to mark the revolver in her hand.

My God, she thought, appalled at the possible consequences. *I could have shot you!*

Realising the danger, she quickly engaged the safety catch and placed the revolver carefully in her pocket. She turned back to the house and was aware once again that there appeared to be no one around. The knot in her stomach tightened and she began to wonder if it would be wise to return to the car and drive off.

Don't be ridiculous, Carla! she told herself. *Collect Monique and get back to Scott.*

She quickly surveyed the grounds again, but there was still no sign of any other human presence.

Wherever are you, Monique, and where the hell's that bloody stupid policeman when I need him?

Her anxiety was heightened by the emptiness of Pimaquet and she didn't know why, but she suddenly found herself easing Ben's slim mobile phone into one of the concealed compartments of her combat jeans. Walking towards the front door, she was alerted again by a sudden rustling behind her. Assuming it was the police guard, she spun round. There was no one there and the cat had disappeared. She turned back and made her way towards the front door. Suddenly, a flock of small birds flew out on mass from a tree at the side of the house. The noise was surprisingly deafening, almost causing her to jump out of her skin. Turning sharply, she could see nothing that could have caused the creatures to have taken flight in such alarm. Then, the eerie silence returned. There was more crunching of dried vegetation and the cold, clammy sweat renewed itself on her body, making her shiver unnaturally in the hot Provençal sun. Carla, now very frightened, ran over to the house. Reaching the front door, she hesitated apprehensively for a few seconds, briefly wondering why Monique hadn't been looking out for her.

'Monique!' she shouted into the building. 'Where are you? We need to get back to Draguignan.'

There was no reply and so, taking a deep breath, she cautiously entered the house. The sight that greeted her in the kitchen shocked her to the core. She stared around the room, dumb struck with fright.

'Come on then, let's talk!' snapped Scott.

'Why do you think I'm Foxicat?'

Scott sneered sarcastically. 'Because, you've got traitor written all over your face.'

Pierre smiled, but it wasn't menacing. 'Can I ask you another question, Scott?'

Scott didn't answer.

'How did you find Mombassa in the tropical snow?'

Scott sat up, startled. 'What did you say?'

'You heard the question, Major O'Sullivan.'

'That's code 5e.'

'Why are you so surprised? You were told you would be contacted today.'

'You're the agent in Var?'

'That's correct.'

Scott inwardly cringed as he realised his grave error of judgement. *How could I have been so bloody stupid?* he thought.

'So that explains why your body language wasn't right!' he exclaimed aloud.

Pierre didn't comment. 'What have you found out?'

Scott looked around, took out his mobile phone and checked the de-bug scanner. When he was quite sure the sensor hadn't detected any surveillance monitoring in the room, he asked: 'How secure is this building?'

'I don't know, Scott. CAT is getting more sophisticated and I'm still not sure who their contacts are in my police department.'

'When did you learn about the operation at La Maison?'

'The morning after the attack, I returned to my office to find a message from the UK NCB. They had posted a red notice on all CAT members in Var. The email explained everything and informed me that, by some lucky chance, the brother of the sole survivor was a secret service agent in the British army.'

Scott stared at him. He hadn't expected this.

'I'm sorry to have shocked you, but I couldn't risk taking you into my confidence until I was quite sure we wouldn't be intercepted and I knew you'd be able to access all the necessary information at Pimaquet.'

Scott knew now that there was no further need for any explanation. 'I've wondered for some time when they would attempt a bio-terrorism attack in Europe. How many people in the police department know about this?'

'Only a handful of people that have been cleared by the offices in Lyon,' replied Pierre gravely. 'Interpol obtained evidence that CAT had infiltrated the system and I was enlisted by French intelligence to investigate the police department in Provence. Unfortunately, CAT discovered my true identity and we've been battling with them, unsuccessfully, ever since.'

'So they know that you're a special agent, too. Why didn't you tell me about the other attacks?'

'I decided that if you didn't visit me today, then I would drive over to Pimaquet, implement code 5e and tell you everything. Fortunately, I haven't needed to do that.'

Scott nodded. Now he understood.

'Carla will be safe at the hospital, so I need you to tell me everything you've discovered.'

Scott assumed Carla would be on her way back from Pimaquet, so he didn't feel the need to elaborate on Pierre's supposition. Without wasting any more time, he began his summary.

Carla entered Pimaquet very cautiously and was horrified to find the house had been ransacked. Chairs and tables had been strewn around the room in what appeared to have been a senseless, frenzied fit of temper. She looked around the room, petrified and, for a moment, was unable even to speak. Eventually, she just managed to call out Monique's name, but there was no reply. A flickering movement, detected briefly in the corner of her eye, made her freeze once more. Realising she wasn't alone, beads of cold sweat popped up all over the surface of her skin and her heart raced painfully, as terror took grip for a second time. Her stomach churned and icy shudders shook her body, as she slowly turned to confront the gruesome abomination. As expected, it wasn't Monique. Carla started to scream.

Scott was coming to the end of his account. Pierre listened, appalled.

'You did what? You went to that house, without proper backup, knowing full well how dangerous these people are?'

'Well, if you had revealed yourself to me properly, I wouldn't have needed to take the additional risk, would I?'

'We assumed you could look after yourself and wouldn't do anything stupid!' He paused before asking: 'Did you discover anything significant there?'

Scott explained how he had hidden under the step and witnessed boxes being brought out of the house. He described the woman lighting the cigarette and how he had identified her as Sarah Radley.

Pierre listened in shock, as he described the visit with Carla and Monique the next day. 'I was in your house when you got back and you didn't tell me!'

'I thought you might be Foxicat! I couldn't risk alerting CAT.'

Pierre sighed and admitted: 'It looks like you're not the only one who misjudged the situation. I should have spoken to you sooner!'

'I don't think that matters now. What can you tell me about Paul Barle and his theories about Freemasons?'

For the first time in their discussion Pierre was able to laugh. 'You went to see Paul Barle, after all?'

Scott nodded.

'What did you think of him?'

'He has some very strange ideas.'

'He does indeed, but I can assure you that there isn't a Masonic connection. Paul Barle is a fanatic and his theories are crazy.'

Pierre paused for a moment, focussing his mind back to Scott's revelations.

'Obviously they're still using La Maison, so we need to collect Carla from the hospital and significantly increase the guard at Pimaquet.'

He saw the awkward look on Scott's face.

'What is it?' he asked urgently.

'Pierre, Carla isn't actually at the hospital.'

'Where is she then?'

'She's driven over to Pimaquet to collect Monique Ribert.'

'Why's she done that?'

Scott put his head in his hands and looked up towards Pierre.

'We didn't only go to the hospital to see Ben this morning. We went to a meeting with Jean-Jacques Broqua.'

Pierre looked alarmed. 'Oh no, please tell me that Jean-Jacques Broqua doesn't know anything about you.'

'I'm afraid I told him about Sarah Radley.'

'*Nom de Dieu*! When did she leave?'

'She dropped me off here and then drove straight over to Bargemon.'

Pierre looked at his watch, 'So she should be on her way back now.'

'Yes,'

'That hire car of yours is chipped, so at least we'll be able to trace it.'

He quickly called up the relevant programme on the computer and used the satellite navigation system to locate the car.

'Shit, it's still at Pimaquet!' He activated the communicator on his desk and scrambled a message. 'I need a team of armed men in Bargemon. I want them to meet me at Pimaquet immediately.'

He turned to Scott. 'Do you have a gun?'

'I gave it to Carla when she left for Bargemon.'

Pierre leapt up and went over to a locked cabinet. He opened it, took out a 32ACP calibre Browning 1910 pistol, checked it was loaded and handed it to Scott.

'Come with me,' he ordered.

Scott followed and they left the building.

They arrived at Pimaquet with a van of armed police. Everything seemed quiet and normal as they jumped out of the car and made their way towards the kitchen.

'*Fouillez le parc!*' Pierre ordered to two of the guards, who headed off immediately to search the grounds.

The front door was wide open. Having received no response to their calls, Scott and Pierre entered the house. They went into the kitchen and Scott experienced waves of nausea as the over powering stench of vomit, urine and excrement made him wretch. The room was uncannily dark, all the shutters had been closed and there was no response from the light switches. Scott tripped over a large carving knife that had been flung thought-lessly onto the floor. It was stained with blood. Then they saw a body, tossed insignificantly in one corner of the room. It was surrounded by a pool of urine and vomit. Pierre and Scott went over to the corpse. It was Monique Ribert and she had been shot in the head.

'Oh my God,' shouted Scott, and frantically called out Carla's name.

There was no response.

Two policemen came into the room and informed them that they had found the body of the guard in the grounds. He had been shot at close range. There was no sign of Carla.

Scott was shaking with rage as he returned with Pierre to the police station in Draguignan. He sat in Pierre's office, mulling over the latest development.

'This is my fault! I shouldn't have let Carla collect Monique alone.'

Pierre was about to reply as his desk phone rang. He answered it and listened carefully to the voice at the other end of the line. He replaced the receiver and said: 'That was the laboratory. Scott, do you know Carla's blood group?'

'Group O. She's a universal donor.'

'Are you sure?'

'Yes. I remember the three of us discussing our blood groups when I first met her, but you can check it with the hospital.'

'That's encouraging. The blood we found on the carving knife in the kitchen was group AB. Monique Ribert was the same as her parents': group A.'

Scott cringed at the use of past tense to describe Monique Ribert.

'So the blood on the knife must have been from one of the people who abducted your sister-in-law.'

'Well, I hope he's bleeding to death!'

'That's a bit gender-specific,' replied Pierre dryly. 'It could quite easily be a woman.'

Scott looked up, his head flashing images of the woman smoking a cigarette and the photograph on Carla's phone. He got up and went over to Pierre's desk.

'Pierre, call up the medical history of Sarah Radley.'

'Why?'

'I need to see her blood group, but I think I already know the answer.'

'I don't see how that can be of any help at all.'

'Blood group AB is very rare, less than three per cent of the population have it. I want to see if the blood on the knife matches with her.'

Pierre went over to his monitor, and accessed the medical records for Sarah Radley. He clicked on the blood group icon. When the information flashed on the screen Scott stood back, satisfied with the result.

BLOOD GROUP: AB RHESUS POSITIVE.

'It's a coincidence,' said Pierre at last.

'I don't think so! When I said the woman I saw at the house was identical to Sarah Radley, everyone told me it was just a coincidence. Then I discovered she had a blood alcohol level of forty per cent and six hundred milligrams of temazepam in her blood. I said it was impossible for her to have ingested that quantity, but everyone else was convinced she had committed suicide. Now we've discovered that one of the people who abducted Carla tonight is blood group AB. Sarah Radley is also blood group AB and you still say it's a coincidence. Come on, Pierre, there are too many bloody coincidences!'

Pierre looked at Scott, his mind quickly trying to put together all the pieces.

'Very well,' he said eventually. 'We'll exhume the body immediately.'

Nine

They drove to the cemetery with an armed convoy. As they arrived, Pierre received confirmation that Jean-Jacques Broqua had disappeared.

'Sod it!' cursed Scott. 'I obviously tipped him off.'

'There's an international red alert out so don't worry, we'll get him!'

At the cemetery, Pierre had made all the necessary arrangements. The coffin had been excavated and placed by the side of the grave. The seal was removed and, with mounting trepidation, they peered into it. Inside the coffin was a bag of sand.

'I knew it,' said Scott, as triumphantly as he could muster. 'She didn't drink all that alcohol and OD on temazepam. Sarah Radley is still alive and working for CAT, which is why Broqua fabricated the autopsy report.'

Pierre turned angrily to one of the police officers. 'Arrest everybody at those undertakers and get the names of any individual who came into contact with the body, at any level. Detain and interrogate them under the powers of *association de malfaiteur*. I'll take full responsibility!'

'Does that include policemen, sir?'

'Yes!'

Scott looked impressed. 'So they won't be charged, or put on trial and they'll stay in prison for as long as it takes to get some answers?'

'Some of them will.' He turned back to his police officer. 'Do it immediately.'

As the officer left to carry out his orders, Scott shrugged and added: 'I wish our government would have the guts to introduce legislation like that.'

'Well, Scott, in the rest of Europe we all feel very let down by the United Kingdom. It's hard for us to understand, for example, why your intelligence network permitted that cleric in north-west London to preach his hatred for so long. It was obvious that he was recruiting suicide bombers. I'm convinced that most of our internal problems occur because your government won't clamp down on radicals.'

'Tell me about it!'

Pierre smiled ruefully, realising that they held the same views on politics. He returned his attention back to the empty coffin.

'I'm still finding all of this very hard to comprehend. I saw the body at La Maison with my own eyes. The woman wasn't breathing and her body was cold.'

'Did you touch her?'

Pierre thought for a moment, desperately trying to retrace all his movements.

'No, I don't think I did; but she must have been because Jean-Jacques said…'

He tailed off.

'Exactly. Because Dr Broqua said her body was cold – and you believed him.'

'I had no reason not to believe him! He's our chief pathologist, for God's sake!'

'He was under suspicion, wasn't he?'

'There wasn't any evidence directly linking him to CAT; it was all just supposition.'

'Even so, don't you have a system for monitoring death certificates?'

'Of course!' said Pierre, irately. 'But, the aftermath of the storm had stretched all our resources to breaking point. The hospital in Draguignan isn't large and was overwhelmed with injuries from the mudslide, not to mention the six people who were murdered. We didn't have the time, or need, to double-check every piece of information.'

'No, I suppose not,' conceded Scott. 'The people who were

involved with handling the body were obviously either working for, or paid off by, CAT.'

'It's more likely they were threatened. You know how CAT operates; they're worse than the mafia.'

'That's true, so expect to find a wall of silence with the people you arrest!'

'The interrogation process will get some answers; you can be sure of that. What about Sarah Radley: how did she become involved with these terrorists?'

'She was born in Draguignan and brought up in the Middle East, where I assume she fell under the influence of a fanatical Muslim group. They do tend to recruit people when they're young, vulnerable and easily indoctrinated.'

'How did she come to marry Radley?'

'They've been married less than two years. I assume she was instructed to seduce him. Women try it on with me all the time!'

He grinned and Pierre laughed.

'But how could she fake her death?'

'Broqua must have induced a cataleptic coma,' answered Scott.

'How could he do that?'

'Funnily enough, I made a study of this at university. Cataleptic comas can be brought on by a number of stimulants. He must have administered a neuroleptic drug.'

'What?'

'Catalepsy, or behavioural immobility, can be evoked in rats and mice by injecting a dopamine blocker.'

'What the hell's dopamine?'

'It's a neurotransmitter that locks on to specific structures in the nervous system, called active sites. Once attached to the appropriate neurone, it stimulates a chemical reaction that activates the muscle tissue. If you block the appropriate active site with an almost identical compound, such as manidipine, the muscles can't function. As a result, the patient appears to be completely immobile.'

'So this blocker stops the neuroreceptor from working?'

'That's right. They have a similar chemical structure to the original, but aren't isomers, so the neurones controlling muscle contraction aren't switched on.'

'Can this process be reversed?'

'Yes, by administering an anticholinergic agent, such as muscarinic acetylcholine.'

'I see. And how easy is it to get hold of one of these dopamine blockers?'

'Very easy if you have access to a pharmacy store. Neuroleptics, or dopaminergic blockers, are widely used in all fields of medicine. Manidipine, for example, is used to treat hypertension and oxatomide is an anti-histamine.'

Scott stopped in his tracks as he finished the sentence.

'Pierre, I'm a fool! She'd been prescribed chlorphenamine.'

'Scott, now you're losing me.'

'I looked at her medical records last night and discovered she had regular prescriptions of chlorphenamine. Carla said it was probably to treat hay fever, so it'll have anti-histaminic properties. She was cataleptic and that's what the medication was for!'

'Why didn't her medical records confirm that?'

'If I could break into the system, then so could CAT. They must have wiped it.'

'So why didn't they delete the records of the medication, too.'

'Anyone seeing the prescription would assume, as Carla had, that it was for hay fever. Cataleptic epilepsy is still very rare and some physicians still refuse to acknowledge that it even exists.'

Pierre ran his hands through his hair, desperately trying to digest everything Scott had said.

'OK, Scott. For the sake of argument let's assume that you're right and she was taking medication to control catalepsy. To instigate a coma she would need to have taken one of these blockers. Do they have the same effect on humans as they do on rats and mice?'

'I don't know. Rats have a similar metabolism to humans, so there's no reason to assume that it wouldn't work.'

'How do you account for the high levels of drug and alcohol in her blood?'

'Broqua made that up to make it look like a suicide but, fortunately, Carla works in chemical research laboratories and she said it wouldn't be possible to have access to six hundred milligrams.'

'The hospital in St Remy must have given it to her.'

'We can easily check that, but Carla was given custody of the medication and she said Sarah Radley had only been prescribed ten doses of thirty milligrams. So, I think he made a typing error and meant to record sixty milligrams of temazepam. I looked it up on the Web and that quantity would have easily killed her. He was intending to show us the autopsy report tomorrow and I suspect he would have noticed the mistake beforehand and changed it.'

'That's incredible! How did they think they could pull this off?'

'It wouldn't have been that difficult. If you remember, when the police arrived they were confronted with a string of terrible crimes. A woman in a cataleptic coma could easily have gone unnoticed. I'm assuming that all the police officers were genuine.'

'Of course they were!'

Scott smiled at his indignation and permitted him to save face, well aware of Pierre's suspicions within the police department.

'In that case, all Broqua had to do was to ensure her body was kept at a reasonable distance from anyone not involved in the espionage.'

'I think you must be right, Scott. Sarah Radley must have warned Foxicat that there were going to be a number of British intelligence agents at the hotel and they organised their assassinations.'

'So they arranged for Radley to be involved in a fatal accident at Les Baux. Of course, she was fortunate that there was a gust of wind at the moment of the murder but, even if there hadn't been, she could have still made it look like an accident.'

'So they arranged to kill him separately to ensure she had a realistic escape route?'

'It would have been the only way to have made her fake suicide look convincing. She must have been observing everyone very carefully at Les Baux and waited patiently for just the right moment.'

'I suppose if the opportunity hadn't arisen,' added Pierre, 'her husband would have been killed with the other agents in the hotel and she would have disappeared.'

'Who knows? They had everything very well planned and presumably they had organised a number of contingencies.'

'I'm still not totally convinced by this, Scott. Is it really possible to induce a realistic cataleptic coma?'

'You can't create a situation of complete suspended animation using dopamine blockers. Even in the most severe state of catatonia, the heart beats fairly normally and the body temperature doesn't fall by very much. In extreme cases, the limbs become totally rigid and retain their position when moved.'

'Just like rigor mortis?'

'Absolutely. There's no response to any stimuli and there is a total loss of muscle control. Viewed from a distance, it would be quite possible to misdiagnose the condition.'

'But a doctor wouldn't be misled by it?'

'No. Broqua must have carefully organised the work rota to ensure only CAT sympathisers were on day duty in the mortuary during the period the agents were at the hotel. My God, they planned this well!'

'They took a huge risk though,' said Pierre, beginning to understand how it could have happened. 'How would Broqua have vindicated himself if someone not linked to this had noticed her breathing?'

'The body movement would be miniscule and easily missed. He would have been able to account for a misdiagnosis.'

'What about the biological weapons? You said in my office that they were probably stored somewhere in the tunnel before the attack.'

'That's the only explanation for why they moved them the night I saw Radley.'

'Why didn't Ribert tell the agents, so they could apprehend them?'

'It's possible he didn't know. They already suspected him of double-crossing them, or maybe he was just looking after his own interests. After all, Ribert wasn't very trustworthy, was he?'

'No, but why didn't the agents check the tunnel?'

'Your guess is as good as mine. It's possible they didn't have the time; events escalated very quickly after the storm, didn't they?'

'Yes, and they always seem to be one step ahead of us.' He looked at Scott, frustrated. 'You're more experienced in this field than me: what do you suggest we should do next?'

Scott carefully considering all their options.

'We need to change our tactics, Pierre. The only way to defeat them is to put ourselves in their position. What would we do, if we were them?'

'So we need to think like a terrorist?'

'Exactly!'

Pierre looked at Scott with new-found respect as everything began to slot logically into place. When he had first been ordered to cooperate with the British agent he had resented his presence; now he looked upon him as a colleague. He put his arm around Scott and said: 'Scott, you're right. We need to go to visit someone that I know.'

They went back to the car and Pierre drove Scott to St Tropez for a meeting with Marc Bertrand. He was a retired magistrate who had set up the resistance movement in Var after the replacement of the Vichy Government in 1942. Marc Bertrand looked every bit his age, but his faculties and mind were as sharp as they had been when he practised law. When Pierre introduced him to Scott, he sat in a wicker chair – a frail old man looking out over the Mediterranean. He warmly welcomed them and after the necessary protocol, Pierre told him about his suspicions. Marc didn't seem at all surprised to hear that La Maison was involved with the smuggling of weapons. He was, however, very dismissive of Pierre's conclusion that Jean-Jacques Broqua was the notorious Foxicat.

'I think you must be mistaken,' he insisted, almost arrogantly. 'I agree that your evidence does suggest that Broqua is a member of CAT, but he wouldn't be their leader.'

'Why?' asked Scott. 'All the evidence suggests that Broqua is Foxicat.'

'I don't dispute that he's a CAT agent,' continued Marc patronisingly. 'I recruited his father during the war as a scout in the resistance, but he never showed any real leadership potential. The younger Broqua is exactly the same, loyal and hard-working, but he doesn't have the qualities that Foxicat would require to oversee an organisation as powerful as CAT.'

Wouldn't he now? This is a very interesting development, thought

Pierre. *Who would have such qualities, Marc?* 'Well, he's our most likely suspect at the moment,' he said aloud.

Marc laughed before asking: 'You haven't come here to ask me about the merits of Broqua. What is it you really want from me, Pierre?'

Scott watched him vigilantly. He appeared to be frail, but his mind was fully functional and attentive.

'They've gone into hiding and have taken an English woman as a hostage,' said Pierre. 'We think Broqua might be using similar techniques to those that were adopted by the resistance during the war. You ran the organisation here, Marc. Where would you retreat to if you suddenly needed to disappear?'

'The obvious place would be the bunker.'

'Bunker?' said Pierre, more as a question rather than a statement.

Marc smiled and his whole face lit up, transforming his whole persona into that of an alert soldier.

'The tunnel at La Maison is much more than it seems on first inspection. When it was originally constructed, the planners used the faults in the rock structure to organise a number of tributaries. Each of them was connected to several possible escape routes. There was a cavern in one of the fault lines and it was converted into a large bunker with its own water and air supplies. Only a handful of people are aware of its existence and even fewer know how to access it.'

He laughed with arrogant pride as he recalled the dark days of occupation.

'The Germans did find one of the entrances to the main tunnel, but we had blocked off all the important sections and they were never able to access the genuine escape routes. We even built a false secret hideaway and exit. The Gestapo watched it for nearly two years and didn't catch anyone. They were so stupid!'

Yes, I've been very stupid too haven't I? thought Pierre, before asking, 'So where exactly is this bunker, Marc?'

'It's positioned right under that house.'

'La Maison!' exclaimed Scott. 'So that's where they are.'

'It's certainly the most obvious place,' said Marc, glancing towards Pierre.

'Hmm,' Pierre said, more to himself than anyone else. 'So they won't be there, then.'

Marc laughed again, as Scott looked on in confused anguish. 'What do you mean?' He wanted to leave immediately to find the bunker. 'It's obvious they're hiding there.'

'Broqua knows how the resistance functioned, Scott. I bet most CAT members in Var have links with the old resistance movement.' He was looking directly at Marc as he spoke. 'They'll have been trained not to do things that are obvious. Think of your own military training. They're probably right under our noses as I speak.'

Marc smiled.

'OK, Marc,' asked Pierre cautiously. 'If you were Foxicat, where would you hide out?'

Scott's right, thought Pierre. *I need to think like a terrorist and it's beginning to pay off.*

'Do you know where the Gestapo headquarters was based round here?'

'Castellane, wasn't it?'

'*Très bon, t'es bien informé.* What else do you know about Castellane?'

'It's the entrance to Gorge du Verdon and right on the edge of the Alps. There's a monastery perched on the top of an inaccessible escarpment and the Gestapo took it over during the war.'

'It's also the gateway to Italy, Switzerland and Austria,' Marc interjected.

'Of course, and the mountain beneath it is riddled with caverns and grottos.'

'That's right, Pierre. We built up a whole escape network through those tunnels, right under the Gestapo headquarters. Very few people knew the actual location and Broqua's father was one of them.'

'This does make military sense,' interrupted Scott. 'You set up a base in the one place the enemy wouldn't think of looking.'

'That's right, Monsieur O'Sullivan.'

Think like a terrorist, thought Pierre again. *Of course, it's so obvious! All this time and I never realised. Well, well! They've been very clever. Thank goodness Scott made me think this way!*

'So, all we have to do is locate their headquarters in Castellane,' replied Scott.

'Exactly,' answered Marc. 'Of course, now it's a busy tourist attraction and the last place you would think of looking for an armed terrorist group.'

'You think Broqua would have taken my sister-in-law there?'

'It's the most likely place. Once they feel safe, they'll be able to use one of the many exits to slip into Italy and then over to Africa.'

That's right, keep ahead of your enemy, thought Pierre.

As they left, Marc Bertrand watched them carefully, very pleased with his morning's work, but not as pleased as Pierre Mauron.

'I hoped Marc would give me all the answers I wanted,' said Pierre as they drove back to Draguignan.

'And did he?'

'Oh, yes. Scott, we need to return to police headquarters and make some arrangements.'

Scott looked at him, wondering what he had in mind. When they were back in his office, Pierre explained everything.

Ten

In the ransacked kitchen of Pimaquet, Carla only had time to scream once as she turned to see two hooded CAT soldiers closing in on her. As one of them lurched towards her, she threw herself at full strength towards the overturned kitchen table. The shock of seeing the vandalised room, coupled with the panic of the moment, made her completely forget that she had Scott's gun in her pocket. She'd noticed a knife that had fallen onto the floor and grabbed desperately at it. One of the attackers was almost on top of her and she was only just able to turn and slam the blade forcibly into the aggressor's arm. The pitch of the voice, screaming out in pain, revealed that the assailant was female and the injured terrorist dropped back momentarily, as Monique was dragged into the room and thrown violently onto the floor. For a second, Carla was distracted, enabling another masked gunman to smack her to the ground and kick her ruthlessly over to Monique's cowering body. One man levelled a gun at the two petrified women and moved closer to them as two more hooded guards entered the room.

'Where's the man?' he asked aggressively, in English.

They didn't answer. He signalled to one of the guards, who went over to Monique, picked her up by the hair and, ignoring her screams, slapped her face violently several times before releasing her and kicking her in the stomach. She was pushed back to sprawl in her own urine and vomit. Carla watched in terrified horror whilst Monique vomited again.

'Let's start again,' said the leader maliciously. 'Where is Monsieur O'Sullivan?'

'I don't know,' Carla replied through gritted teeth.

'Oh, I think you do,' he replied. 'Would you like me to start on you?'

'You can do what you like to me, you bastards! I won't tell you anything.'

He nodded over to his accomplices. Two hooded gunmen grabbed Monique and dragged her kicking and screaming to the overturned kitchen table. They picked it up and one of the captors held Monique against it, whilst the other forced her hand onto the surface and held up a cleaver. Monique screamed, completely panic-stricken, soiling herself and urinating again.

The leader addressed Carla. 'You have five seconds to tell me where the man is. If you refuse, we will cut off each of these bitch's fingers in turn. Eventually, you will tell me everything that I need to know!'

Monique gagged, but her stomach was empty. Straining painfully to bring up green bile increased the pressure in her cranium considerably and both eyeballs almost popped out of their sockets. Blood vessels pounded loudly in her head and she watched in shock as the cleaver was placed on the first finger to be amputated. Knowing full well that CAT was unaccustomed to making idle threats, she shouted: 'Stop! You can't do this to me!'

The interrogator came over and looked straight into her eyes.

'You said—' she started to say, but was instantly silenced by a harsh slap across the face.

'Shut up, Ribert! You won't get a second warning!'

He turned back to Carla, who was too shocked to have noticed the exchange between her tormentor and Monique. 'I'll ask you one more time and then I will count to five. Where is the man? One, two—'

'Alright, alright!' Carla screamed in demoralised terror. 'He's gone to see Pierre Mauron.'

'Good girl,' he replied sarcastically. 'Why has he gone to see the Chief of Police?'

Carla looked over at Monique. She knew that she didn't have any choice other than to answer their questions.

'To tell him everything we know,' she said dejectedly.

'When will he be back?'

'I don't know.'

'Cut the first finger off,' he ordered.

Monique screamed out again, causing Carla to go to pieces.

'He's not coming back!' she yelled.

Their interrogator looked at her, his eyes betraying that he was slightly troubled by her response. 'What do you mean, "he's not coming back"? What's he doing?'

Carla knew she had to answer. 'I'm supposed to be taking Monique back to the police station.'

She burst into tears and the amputation was temporarily halted. Monique was left sprawled across the table, also sobbing frenziedly and she was able to sink down to the floor and curl up in a protective ball.

'We'll have to change our plan,' said the woman, holding on tightly to her injured arm. Carla looked over to her, startled, as she recognised the voice. 'If Mauron believes O'Sullivan, they'll send over an armed convoy.'

Carla heaved a sigh of relief. At least Scott would be safe. The leader took off his balaclava and Carla gasped in horror as Jean-Jacques Broqua came over to her.

'It's you!' she just managed to say, through her anger and terror. 'Scott was right: you were Foxicat all along!'

'You compliment me. I'm afraid that I'm not Foxicat; just one of his employees. What a shame you and that pretty-boy companion didn't do as I said this morning.'

'Scott doesn't take orders from scum like you!'

Broqua stared at her intently. His probing eyes invaded her private psyche, making her inwardly squirm with revulsion. 'If you speak to me like that again, I'll order these men to reconstruct your lovely little face!'

She was under no illusion that he was prepared to carry out his threat, but she retorted bravely: 'And then rip out my intestines and wrap them around my neck?'

'I might do exactly that if it becomes necessary. Just remember, with me off the scene for a while, these men could do with the practice!'

His eyes continued to cut into her subconscious with surgical precision. She shuddered and looked away.

He turned to one of the guards. 'Search her.'

Carla was quickly frisked and Scott's gun and the mobile phone removed. Broqua took the gun and examined it. He turned directly to Carla.

'This weapon is used by UK NCB agents. How did you manage to be in possession of one?'

Carla didn't answer.

Broqua thought carefully for a few seconds. 'I'm beginning to wonder if the rumours we've been hearing about your brother-in-law have some substance, but we haven't the time to go into that right now. We'll interrogate you fully when we get back to base. It's unfortunate that you became involved in this, Madame O'Sullivan. You should have stayed in the hospital with your husband, but now it's too late.'

Although terrified, Carla was unable to contain her anger any further.

'How could I not have become involved? You tried to murder my husband and planned to kill hundreds of innocent people in Britain.'

Broqua shook his head. 'I wouldn't listen too carefully to what O'Sullivan has told you about us; CAT doesn't carry out terrorist attacks. We just supply the merchandise.'

'It's the same thing! Can't you see that?'

The woman came over to her and removed the balaclava covering her face. Carla recognised her immediately and although she had recognised the voice, the actual revelation still shocked her to the core.

'Sarah! Scott did see you after all!'

She smiled malevolently and there was no mistaking the fanaticism in her face. Her arm was still bleeding from the knife attack and she ripped up part of the table covering and tied it tightly around the wound, using it as a tourniquet.

'Broqua's right, Carla. We just assist all the oppressed people in the world. I saw exactly how the West treats Muslims when I lived in the Middle East with my parents. Now it's time for them to fight back. You'll understand when you meet them.'

Carla shook her head in contempt.

'Never, and there is no justification for what you're trying to do!'

'You've been brainwashed by capitalist shit. When you see it for yourself, you'll change your mind.'

'I will not and you're the one whose been indoctrinated, not me. Ben's brother will sort you out!'

'Don't be ridiculous!' she replied viciously, the phrenetical devotion sparkling dangerously in her eyes. 'Do you realise how powerful this organisation is? We sell arms and drugs to terrorist groups all over the world. No one can stop us!'

'There's an armed guard in the grounds and he'll contact the police in Draguignan,' sobbed Monique.

Carla was suddenly inexplicably unnerved and alarmed by Monique's words. They sounded more like a warning than a threat.

Broqua laughed and replied. 'You don't need to worry about him – he's dead. We killed him, just as we did your treacherous father!'

'Why are you doing this?' Monique screamed. 'You promised that if I did what you asked, everything would be alright!'

Carla spun round. 'What did you say?'

Monique was silent and looked shamefully down to the floor. Carla stared at her. A nauseous feeling of anger took root, as the ultimate betrayal caused the last vestige of decency and honour to abandon her. She choked on her words and only just managed to ask: 'I trusted you and all the time you've been working with CAT. Why?'

Monique was still sobbing as she answered. 'They made me, Carla! I didn't have any choice. I'm so sorry.'

'Of course you had a choice!'

'I didn't, Carla. They said—'

'Shut up!' interrupted Radley.

She went over to Monique's crouching body and kicked her violently in the head. The assault stunned her, causing her head to spin and she passed out.

Radley looked down contemptuously at Monique and said to Broqua: 'I've had enough of this bitch! She didn't inform us about O'Sullivan's investigation as we ordered. This Ribert is as unreliable as the other two and we only need one of them as a hostage, Jean-Jacques.'

Broqua nodded in agreement. She raised her gun and shot Monique through the head. Blood splattered over the wall with a sickening thud. Carla shook with rage. Fear had suddenly evaporated. She looked at Monique's callous killer and knew there was no hope.

Her voice cracked as she said defiantly: 'My husband and brother-in-law will track you down. You'll never escape their vengeance!'

'But, of course, first Ben has to wake up, doesn't he?' retorted Sarah. 'And with our contacts in the hospital it will be so easy to poison his drip and then fake the autopsy report!'

They both sniggered.

'I'll quickly mark Ribert,' said Broqua.

Radley stopped him. 'No, there isn't time. We can't risk O'Sullivan arriving back here with the police or the army.'

Broqua knew she was right and turned to the guards, gesturing towards Carla. 'Take her to the car.'

She tried to put up resistance, but her abductors were too strong. They dragged her outside where a limousine with blackened windows had silently materialised. She was roughly blindfolded and positioned between two armed men in the back of the car. It drove off at high speed. She had no idea how long her journey lasted, but eventually they came to a halt. She was dragged out, still blindfolded. Her terror was heightened by the disorientation, but the sudden change of air made her realise she had been taken into a building. She was pushed violently into what she thought must be a chair and she heard Broqua say in French: 'We've brought this woman to hold as a hostage, sir.'

'What happened?' replied a male voice that she didn't recognise.

'O'Sullivan has gone to see the Chief of Police,' he answered. 'We disposed of the guard and had to kill Monique Ribert. She became unreliable, like her parents.'

He didn't give a second's thought to the fate of Monique. 'Didn't you say the man thought Mauron was Foxicat?'

'Yes, sir, but he must have changed his mind.'

'Very well,' said the alien voice. 'You've done the right thing.'

Carla understood very little of the conversation, but became bolder as fear transformed into anger.

'I assume that I'm in the presence of Foxicat,' she said in English, turning as far as she could in the direction of her abductor's voice.

'You are very well informed,' he replied, in perfect English. 'My code name is Foxicat France.'

'I want to see your face.'

Foxicat laughed.

'Only selected members of CAT can see my face. Anyone else would have to die.'

'I'm going to be killed anyway, aren't I?' she answered courageously.

'Maybe. It depends on just how useful you turn out to be,' he replied and then spoke to his employees in French. 'Broqua, lock her up securely.'

She was bundled away violently and thrown down a flight of steps. She hit the cold stone floor at the bottom with a painful thump that almost knocked her unconscious. In her delirium she thought she heard the footsteps of her abductors following her. She was suddenly dragged up and forced along a corridor. Keys rattled in the background and she heard one engage in a lock. A door opened, she was pushed into a room and the blindfold ripped from her face. It took some time to get accustomed to the dim light coming from a single light bulb hanging from the stone ceiling. The door was slammed shut and she heard it being locked. Falling onto a bare mattress, she looked around the room hardly able to discern what was happening. There were no windows in the small bare prison. It was dank, clammy and she didn't have any blankets to keep her warm. Huddled up on the damp, lumpy mattress, she wondered if she would ever see the light of day again. Looking at her watch, she noted it was just after three o'clock.

The time passed excruciatingly slowly. It was cold and she couldn't sleep. She lay terrified on the mattress for over three hours before she heard the sound of movement outside the door. The key turned in the lock and Broqua entered the room accompanied by two armed guards.

'I should make the most of these,' said Broqua, as one of the guards threw some blankets onto the floor. The other terrorist gave her a thermos flask containing soup and a bottle of water.

'What's going to happen to me?'

'In a little while you're coming with us to Africa. You'll be a very useful hostage.'

'What will happen when we get to Africa?'

'That very much depends on you and how cooperative you can be. Our contacts have informed us that you're a chemical analyst. That skill could be very helpful to us.'

'I'll never cooperate with you!'

'We shall see.'

'The police will come and get me,' she said, only half-believing what she was saying.

'I don't think so. We know every move they make!'

He left the room and she sank back down in despair. In the solitude of her lonely confinement, tears flowed freely.

Eleven

Security was noticeably increased around the police buildings as Scott and Pierre, along with a hastily assembled working party, sought approval for their complex and daring manoeuvre. They communicated and received instructions from the general secretary of Interpol in Lyon using the messenger programme on Scott's mobile phone.

YOU HAD BETTER BE RIGHT ABOUT THIS, 5903.

Scott looked up, 'We're taking a huge risk, Pierre. If our intelligence turns out to be wrong and we invade an innocent civilian's house, we'll both be finished!'

'Scott, we've talked this through and have both reached the same conclusion. All we have to do is follow our scheme and trust that the marines can do the rest.'

'It's still mainly based around your instinct though and I'd feel much easier using the British marines who I'm accustomed to working with!'

'The President would not have allowed foreign soldiers to take military action on French soil! Can you imagine the public outrage if the media picked up the story?'

Scott banged his hand on the table in frustration. 'Politicians! They make me sick! Here we are trying to avert a major terrorist attack and all they are worried about is public opinion!'

'That's how it is, as well you know!'

Scott shrugged. 'Did you get any useful information from the undertakers?'

'No. I forgot to tell you: they've disappeared.'

'All of them?'

'Yes, but it was a small family business.'

'I bet it was! What about the hospital?'

'Broqua's assistant has disappeared and all we've managed to detain are some very frightened technicians and porters.'

'Are you interrogating them?'

'Of course, but I don't think they know anything. Foxicat has ensured we've only been left with the small fry.'

'Fuck them and their efficiency!'

They were interrupted by a police officer who came into the office and handed Pierre a piece of paper. He looked at it, smiled and went over to Scott.

'Have a look at this document. I think it will finally convince you that we've made the right decision.'

'What is it?' asked Scott as he took the paper from Pierre.

'It's a copy of Radley's death certificate. Look at the second verification signature.'

Scott studied it. 'It's signed by Marc Bertrand!'

'Exactly. He may be retired, but he still acts in an official capacity for the district of Var from time to time. In this case, he was the coroner!'

'How the fuck did they think they'd get away with that?'

'They probably assumed that no one would suggest that she had risen from the dead!'

Scott shook his head. 'Alright, you've convinced me, Pierre!'

He turned back to the computer screen.

We are 100% sure we have identified Foxicat France as Marc Bertrand and we believe the missing consignment is with him.

The reply was quick to come back.

OK. YOU HAVE CLEARANCE. GOOD LUCK.

Scott turned back to Pierre.

'Well, that's it. All we have to do now is come up with the goods!'

As they were preparing to leave, the phone rang. Pierre took the call.

'It's the hospital,' he said to Scott and then listened to the voice on the other end, as the British agent hovered over him anxiously.

'I'm afraid they won't be able to come to the hospital until tomorrow,' he said into the receiver. He put the phone down and turned to Scott.

'Your brother has regained consciousness.'

The relief on Scott's face was indescribable. 'Thank God! How is he?'

'They've done a scan that indicates there's no lasting damage to his nervous system. He'll just need rest, some physiotherapy and a lot of love. They've moved him out of ICU and into a ward. Apparently he's able to speak quite coherently and is complaining that you and Carla aren't there! So, that's some good news for you, at last.'

'I don't suppose I can go and see him quickly?'

'No, I'm sorry, Scott. Have you forgotten that we've imposed a security blackout?'

'No, of course not, but surely I can ring him?'

'He hasn't got his mobile phone has he? And anyway, how would you explain why Carla isn't with him at the hospital?'

Scott didn't answer. He knew it was impossible to contact Ben. His brother would have to wait until the morning.

When it was dark, Pierre and Scott left the building. In the foothills overlooking the police headquarters, CAT's surveillance observed them through powerful Bushnell night vision binoculars. They watched the car pull away and used mobile phones to contact the next look out along the line. Throughout the length of the chain from Draguignan to Callas, the CAT contacts telephoned in their reports as the car passed through each of the lookout points.

Pierre drove steadily, knowing full well that he was being carefully scrutinised at every stage of the route. Their anxiety was heightened as they drove through Callas and joined the mountainous road leading to Bargemon. It was here that their plan could go disastrously wrong. There was one small stretch of road that provided a blind spot to the gang's infrared equipment and it was at this point that the scheme could either succeed or fail. The timing was perfect as they met an undercover police car that had been travelling in the opposite direction. Quickly, they exchanged vehicles. The occupants of the second car were dressed identically to Pierre and Scott. Within seconds they had swapped cars and their replicas were back on the road, travelling at the same speed towards Castellane as the two agents before the changeover.

Scott and Pierre continued their journey in their new vehicle in the opposite direction. A few moments later, another black car passed them in hot pursuit of the facsimiles. They had made the exchange just in time. The planning team had suspected Foxicat would have organised alternative supervision on the barren section of road leading to Bargemon and the substitution had been executed faultlessly.

Pierre now drove quickly and within the hour they had reached their true destination. He parked the car and they made the last section of their journey to Marc Bertrand's house on foot. They knew exactly what had to be done and their time management was, again, absolutely essential. Scott stole silently around the grounds and finally found a window left carelessly open. After successfully breaking into the house, he was relieved to find the room was empty and in darkness. He crept over to the door and, on hearing voices, made a quick dash for a large table covered to the floor with a white cotton cloth. It concealed his body just in time, as the door opened and two people entered the room. Scott recognised Marc Bertrand's voice immediately. When he finally dared to peep out from under the table, he wasn't surprised to see that Bertrand was speaking to Sarah Radley.

'We fooled them nicely,' she said to Marc. 'The lookouts are following the Chief of Police and that idiot Englishman all the way to Castellane.'

'I wouldn't underestimate Monsieur O'Sullivan, Radley. The gun taken from the woman in the cellar has been positively identified as property of the UK division of the National Central Bureau. So, we were right, he does work for British intelligence.'

'I'm not underestimating him, which is why I think we should evacuate these premises as soon as possible.'

'We'll be able to move out in a couple of hours.'

'We should leave now, sir. Once O'Sullivan realises what's

happened they'll send reinforcements and we don't have enough resources here to hold off the army.'

'I doubt if they'll come here. They'll assume I was mistaken and try to find the bunker at La Maison. By the time they discover that it doesn't exist, we'll have leaked out the news about the yesterday's killing at Pimaquet and, with the assistance of our friends in the media, Pierre will be fighting to save his job.'

'So we're keeping to our original arrangements?'

'The boat won't get to us for another two hours. We can't bring that time forward, but tomorrow we'll have arrived safely in Morocco with the merchandise. Once there, we can organise for it to be transported into Britain via the Spanish route.'

'What about that woman?'

'She'll be secure in the cellar until we're ready to move out.'

Scott could hardly believe his luck. The programme of action was working out perfectly. He had confirmation that the consignment was somewhere in the house and Carla was safely locked in the cellar. After consulting his watch, he waited patiently until suddenly, exactly on cue, the electricity supply was cut and the house was plunged into darkness.

'What's going on?' demanded Foxicat.

Jean-Jacques entered the room with a torch.

'There's been a huge power failure. It looks like the whole of St Tropez has been affected.'

'Excellent. We couldn't have organised this any better,' said Foxicat. 'The blackout will give us just the right amount of cover to enable us to slip out of France undetected.'

'I hope you're right,' replied Radley. 'My instinct is that we should move out now and meet the boat at sea.'

'You're getting too jumpy,' added Broqua. 'Mauron is convinced that I'm Foxicat and that our base is in Castellane. We must wait for the boat to pick us up as planned.'

'It's not Mauron that I'm concerned about. He's just been recruited onto this from the police force, whereas O'Sullivan is a trained army agent. He won't be fooled by our ruse for very long!'

'Exactly,' replied Broqua. 'If they do suspect anything then there'll be surveillance on Marc's yacht. We have to wait for our transport from Marrakech.'

They left the room and Scott was able to make his next move. He retrieved a pair of N-Force Viper night vision goggles from his backpack and attached them firmly to his head. The high-resolution lenses gave him perfect vision in the dark, enabling him to find his way easily to the door. Once in the entrance hall, he followed Pierre's instructions and soon found himself at the door leading to the basement. He opened it gingerly, ensuring he made as little sound as possible and made his way carefully down the steps. At the bottom of the stone stairs he could hear nothing. There were several doors leading off the main section but only one was shut. He looked in each of the open rooms and eventually saw two cases. Hoping it was the consignment of biological weapons, he warily moved over to one of the boxes and gently prised it open. It appeared to be full of bubble wrap. He rifled through the packaging fastidiously and was surprised to discover it contained just one metal canister, which he estimated weighed around six kilograms. He took it out of the wrapping. It was cylindrical, approximately one litre in volume and constructed from a heavy metal, which he assumed was lead. It had a faded label, with writing in Russian, but he could clearly discern the symbols ^{239}Pu(94). Scott looked at it in disgust.

'Fuck. It's not anthrax. They're making a dirty bomb!'

He scanned the container with a radiation meter built into his phone and was shocked to see a reading of six thousand becquerels.

'Shit, it's leaking! Don't these morons realise how dangerous this stuff is?'

Scott quickly converted the figure he had measured seeping from the container to the radioactivity level his unprotected body would be absorbing.

'Fuck it, that's one hundred and fifty millisieverts! Not a fatal dose, but enough to affect my body cells!'

After placing the container on the floor he opened the other crate and unwrapped small slabs of semtex and detonators. After inspecting everything vigilantly, he got out his mobile phone.

I've found the consignment. It's not anthrax. It's explosives and plutonium!

The response was almost instantaneous.

Secure it!

The container isn't properly sealed. I got a reading of 6000Bq.

He waited for what seemed an eternity.

That's high, but we can decontaminate you. Get it up here as quickly as you can.

Scott placed the canister of plutonium in his backpack and resealed the empty box in which he had found the deadly arsenal. He left the store room with the container safely in his possession and started to move over to the locked chamber.

Carla spent an uncomfortable evening in her cold prison. She hadn't been fed since late afternoon, although Broqua had brought her a fresh supply of water.
    'You're becoming quite interesting, O'Sullivan,' he said.
    She didn't answer.
    'You're a research chemist and arrived at Pimaquet to collect a friend, armed with a gun used by Interpol special agents. Have you an adequate explanation for that?'
    Again she refused to reply.
    'We were obviously correct to bring you here and, when we get to Africa, CAT has big things planned for you.'
    Carla looked at him coldly. 'I've already told you, I'd rather die than be of any assistance to you!'
    Broqua laughed. 'We shall see. In the end, very few people are able to resist us!'
    He left her to contemplate the future. She wondered how they intended to secure her cooperation. Fear of being tortured flashed through her mind, or perhaps they would subject her to an intensive brainwashing campaign. Whichever option they employed, her immediate future didn't look too bright. Lying back down on the uncomfortable mattress, the hours melded into one timeless void, as her mind scurried over her unenviable fate. She had completely lost track of time when unexpectedly the light

went out. The blackout in the cold dank atmosphere of her prison compounded her misery. In the repressive darkness, Carla could only reflect on the terrifying circumstances that had catapulted her into this nightmare. She had no idea how long she had been lying in the darkness when suddenly there was a noise outside the door. Her heart began to beat rapidly as someone tried the door. The disorientation of her confinement caused her head to fill with further thoughts of despair. Perhaps they had decided to kill her after all. Then there was the voice that she was beginning to lose all hope of ever hearing again.

'Carla, are you in there?'

She could hardly believe it. He called out again and finally she knew it wasn't a cruel hallucination.

'Scott,' she replied quietly, almost crying. 'Is it really you?'

'Thank God you're safe!'

'Please unlock the door and get me out of this terrible place!'

Scott looked at the lock, but there was no key. He scanned the immediate area anxiously, but there was no key to be seen and the door was quite secure.

'There isn't a key down here,' he whispered back to her. 'I'll have to go back upstairs and find it. If it's not in the hall then I'll have to blow the lock off.'

'Can't you do that now?'

'No, Carla. This is far more serious than we first thought. The army are waiting outside for a signal from me. If I shoot the lock off CAT will hear me. That has to be the last resort. We must ensure that both you and the consignment are secured before the attack starts.'

'OK, but be careful Scott! These people are very dangerous. They killed Monique.'

'I know. I found her body.'

With that he had gone and once again she was left alone, but this time the terror was for what might happen to her brother-in-law if he was caught.

Upstairs, there was a flurry of activity as Foxicat ordered his guards into the garden to check the surrounding grounds. The power failure, coupled with Sarah Radley's misgivings, was beginning to make him suspicious and he decided he would feel more comfortable if he had Carla and the consignment under close supervision.

'Broqua, bring the woman up from the cellar and then get some guards to have the consignment ready to move onto the boat.'

The pathologist went out into the hall, using his flashlight to find his way over to the cellar door. He flung it open just as Scott had reached the foot of the stairs. Scott instinctively threw himself back against the wall. As Broqua came down the steps, he dashed back and concealed himself behind one of the open doors. He positioned himself so that he could clearly see the entrance to Carla's prison and watched Broqua approach. The pathologist took a key out of his pocket and unlocked the door. Inside the cell, Carla listened carefully and didn't call out. She was sure that if it was Scott he would have given her a signal. She couldn't risk giving him away. Broqua opened the door and went in.

'Get up!' he ordered.

Scott made his move. He crept quickly over to the prison cell, darted inside and placed a gun into Broqua's back.

'Don't move,' he said in French.

Broqua froze.

'Move over to the wall and turn round.'

Broqua started to move slowly away. He abruptly turned, knocked the gun from Scott's hand and leapt at him. They grappled together frantically for a few seconds, kicking out at each others legs in an attempt to disable their opponent. Scott was highly trained and experienced in unarmed combat, but on this occasion Broqua had the slight advantage as Scott was hampered by his cumbersome night vision goggles. They weighed less than three hundred grams, but weren't designed for one to one warfare and Broqua was quick to realise it. He turned Scott's restricted movement against him and it wasn't long before he began to lose the initiative against the CAT soldier. Scott attempted to rip off his vision aid, but Broqua anticipated his action and kicked out at his legs viciously. Scott fell and Broqua forced the British agent onto his back and smashed his head hard onto the stone floor. The connecting buckle on the back of the glasses cut into the skin at the back of Scott's head, disorientating him. Scott felt firm, rough hands close around his throat and struggled to sit up, but Broqua held him down and continued to smack Scott's head onto the hard floor, destabilising him further. There was little he could do to defend himself against the onslaught. Carla realised this and, as he began to feel consciousness slipping away, she leapt over to the fallen torch and frenziedly used it to locate Scott's pistol. On seeing it in one corner of the cell, she lunged desperately towards the weapon.

Scott was struggling back into the fight as Broqua suddenly realised what Carla was doing. He took his hands away from Scott's throat, kicked out at him and made a dash for her. Scott grabbed his leg and attempted to pull him down, but Broqua was able to drag himself away. Fortunately, Scott's action slowed down the CAT soldier long enough for Carla to reach the revolver. She grabbed it and aimed the torch and the gun at the pathologist.

'Stop or I'll shoot,' she ordered in English.

He instinctively did as he was told. In the blackness of the cellar, the beam from Carla's torch confused him for a few seconds, enabling Scott to quickly roll over and jump to his feet. It took only a few seconds for Broqua to regain his control and he began to move slowly towards Carla.

'You won't shoot me,' he sneered. 'I don't suppose you even know how to use it!'

Scott was about to launch himself at Broqua, using the advantage of his perfect vision, when there was a shot, muffled by the silencer. Broqua fell to the floor, dead. Scott stared at Carla with astonished admiration.

'When did you learn how to shoot like that?'

'Until today I've never fired a gun in my life!'

She ran over to him and they held each other tightly, for a few seconds. He reached into his pocket, took out his mobile and started to activate it.

'What are you doing, Scott?'

'I'm sending the communication to start the attack.'

'Surely your phone won't work in here?'

'They're beaming a booster signal down to me.'

He sent a text message from the template of his mobile's

memory card and after receiving confirmation that it had been delivered, he went over to Broqua's body and kicked it over. Scott riffled quickly through the pathologist's pockets until he found a small handgun.

'Carla, keep hold of my gun. You might need it when the battle starts.'

As he pocketed Broqua's revolver, his mobile phone bleeped.

HAVE U GOT THE PLUTONIUM?

Yes. It's in my backpack.

WELL DONE. YOU HAVE 2 MINS.

'Come on! We need to get out of here fast!'

With Scott armed with Broqua's weapon they moved out of the prison.

After leaving his car, Pierre had made his way towards Marc Bertrand's house, just as Scott had done earlier. He crept round to the side and was able to break into the deserted kitchen and slink into the larder where he knew he could hide undetected. Exactly on time, the pre-arranged power failure occurred. Everything was plunged into darkness. Pierre put on his night vision glasses and waited for the signal that would indicate that Carla had been rescued. Once again, the timing was essential. The attack had to be underway before the two soldiers arrived in Castellane, when it was certain the CAT spies would realise Pierre and Scott had switched vehicles. It wasn't long in coming. A communicator in his pocket bleeped and he read the text from the marines outside.

MATERIAL SECURED. ATTACK IN 2 MINS.

He quickly made his way out of the kitchen and into the hall. As he moved past the entrance to the cellar, he heard a noise and instinctively jumped back. The door creaked gently open. Pierre raised his gun, ready to smash it down on the head of the approaching body. He was just preparing himself to attack when Carla and Scott came through the door. The police chief sighed with relief, issued the gas masks and gave Carla a spare pair of night vision glasses. They quickly explained how to use them as Scott attached the goggles to her head and switched them on. When they were sure Carla was ready, they began to make their way to the epicentre of the French CAT headquarters.

Marc Bertrand was beginning to wonder why Broqua was taking such a long time to collect Carla from the cellar.

'Shall I go and see?' asked Sarah, who was still feeling uneasy about the power failure.

'Yes.'

As she moved towards the door, the first CS gas canisters exploded in the grounds. She spun instinctively towards the sound and another canister exploded through the window, spraying debilitating needles of glass around the room. Sarah was struck straight in the face. She screamed with pain, as razor-sharp shards ripped into her eyes, blinding her. The gas diffused quickly through the room and Marc Bertrand, also injured from the spraying glass, fell coughing to the floor. Radley heard the sound of movement in front of her and was just about to fire her Kalashnikov in the general direction of the sound when Pierre instinctively fired at her. She fell back, blood oozing from her mouth. Marc Bertrand, now fully aware of what was happening, made an attempt to retrieve the weapon. He was stopped by Scott.

'I wouldn't do that, Bertrand!'

He aimed a gun at Marc and shot out his kneecap. Bertrand fell to the floor, yelling in agony, enabling Scott to kick him ruthlessly into the corner of the room. Pierre pulled Carla over to the immobilised leader, whilst Scott made a dash for the Kalashnikov. He reached it only just in time, as Foxicat's guards came swarming in to protect their leader. He took quick command of the weapon and wiped out the attacking CAT soldiers in seconds. They took a defensive position by Marc Bertrand, Pierre holding the disabled terrorist firmly to the ground. Everything happened at such speed that Carla didn't have the time to feel frightened. She took protection behind Scott, who was operating the Kalashnikov, and waited for the conflict to reach a conclusion.

As Scott had hoped, the CAT mercenaries were no match for

the highly-trained French marines and it wasn't long before the combat was successfully achieved. CAT suffered heavy casualties and did all they could to protect Foxicat, but Scott and Pierre easily held them off with the assistance of the AK-47. Suddenly, the deafening gunfire stopped and there was a few seconds of eerie silence before Scott received a message on his mobile, confirming that the French soldiers had taken control of the house. He sent a reply and the army rushed into the room to secure their safe exit. The battle was over and Foxicat had been taken alive. As the soldiers were about to bundle him out of the room, Scott turned to confront his vanquished enemy.

'When will you people finally realise that terrorism will never succeed? We'll always stop you!'

Bertrand, still in acute pain, looked at him impassively. 'There's another hundred people out there waiting to take my place, O'Sullivan!'

'Yes, and we'll get every one of them.'

'Do you really think that what you do is any better than me?' he sneered. 'How many people have you murdered today?'

Scott turned away contemptuously and ordered the soldiers to take him away. He suddenly remembered Carla. She was standing over and looking down at the bloodied body of Sarah Radley. Scott went over to her and put his arm around her.

She looked up at him. 'Monique was working for CAT.'

'I'm sorry.'

'She didn't tell them about us and that's why they executed her.'

'So there was at least one Ribert who could be trusted, then!'

'They were just victims of their circumstances.'

'Isn't that what all criminals claim?'

Carla didn't answer and they looked back down at Sarah Radley.

'I'll tell you what, Carla. I think she really is dead this time!'

She glanced back up at him, smiled ruefully and allowed him to lead her away.

Twelve

After they had been escorted out of the grounds, Scott went over to the officer in charge of the armed combat and handed over the bag containing the canister of plutonium.

'The explosives and detonators are still in the basement. It'll need to be decontaminated and be careful with the canister in this bag. It's leaking at a rate of six thousand becquerels.'

'Everything's been organised, Major O'Sullivan and we're transporting you both to a decontamination unit at our base in Frejus.'

'I wasn't exposed to it for very long, but I'm concerned about my sister-in-law. She was locked in a room next to the leakage for several hours.'

'She should be alright, Major. It's still a relatively low dose.'

Scott nodded in acknowledgement and then looked at the French major sternly. 'I'm very disturbed about our intelligence being so badly wrong! I was informed that this was a suspected biological attack; instead, they were planning to contaminate London with radioactive waste!'

'We've informed the President and the British prime minister. There will be a secret enquiry, but they've asked me to inform you that they're very grateful for what you've done.'

They saluted each other and Major Malraux left with the canister of plutonium isotope 239.

Carla watched the French soldier carry away the deadly arsenal and asked: 'How the hell did they manage to get hold of it?'

Scott looked at her grimly. 'The canister had a Russian label and we've been aware for some time that a significant quantity of plutonium is missing from Soviet hospitals and power plants.'

'How could that have happened?'

'We believe it occurred when the communist regime collapsed in the late twentieth century. There were no controls during that chaotic period, which allowed some radioactive waste to become unaccounted for. It's been impossible to track, even with satellite observation.'

'My God, that's terrible!'

'The cache we recovered today is just a small drop in the ocean. Believe me, Carla, there's plenty more out there – just waiting to be snapped up!' He turned to Pierre. 'To think I was trying to stop this stuff getting into Iraq and all the time they were attempting to smuggle it into Britain. My God, if this had been successful, it would have been 9/11 all over again!'

Pierre put his arm around him. 'We stopped them, Scott, and that's all that matters.'

He shrugged. 'I wonder if Monique Ribert and all the others who died would agree with you.'

Pierre smiled sympathetically. 'At least your brother is alive and safe.'

'Do you know, during all this, I'd completely forgotten about Ben?' exclaimed Carla. 'Does anyone know how he is?'

Scott turned back to her. 'I'd forgotten about him for a moment, too. They brought him out of the coma just as I was about to come out on this operation.'

Carla couldn't contain her relief or excitement. 'That's wonderful, Scott! I want to go and see him now.'

Scott laughed. 'Have you seen the state of yourself? They wouldn't let you in.'

'I don't care what I look like! I want to go and see him! I mean, we've just saved the bloody world from a nuclear attack; the least they can do is to let me see my husband!'

Major Malraux had returned and was listening to their conversation. He saluted her respectfully and said: 'We've been in contact with the hospital for you, Madame O'Sullivan, and your husband is sleeping peacefully, although it took some time to settle him. He's been complaining that you and Major O'Sullivan haven't been in to visit him.'

Carla laughed. 'I bet he has!'

'You've both been in contact with this material, so we need to get you decontaminated immediately. A helicopter is waiting to transfer you to Frejus.'

'Why didn't you bring a portable unit here?' she asked naively. 'Wouldn't that have been quicker?'

The men all laughed. Carla looked so bemused by their reaction that Scott felt the need to explain. 'They couldn't bring anything like that here and risk the media picking up on it. There are some things that the public just can't be told.'

'So how will you explain about the raid on this house and the murders?'

'I expect Pierre will stick to his cover story about the local coven, whilst encouraging Paul Barle to continue blaming Freemasons!'

'That's about the measure of it,' laughed Pierre.

'As for the raid on this house,' continued Scott, 'it'll be explained away as a crackdown on drugs trafficking, but what really happened over the last few days will have a security blackout for at least the next fifty years.'

'Everything seems to have been well thought out.'

'It has to be in our business, and Carla, you'll be expected to comply with this, too!'

'How can you all be so sure that I wouldn't sell my story to the highest-paying newspaper editor?' she retorted, only half-seriously.

Major Malraux provided the answer. 'All families of special agents are thoroughly vetted – and so, we know you wouldn't do that. Anyway, ma'am, you wouldn't want all your credit to be called in, would you?'

'Or lose your National Insurance number,' added Scott.

Carla stared at them, feeling slightly intimidated. 'How will you explain the disappearance of all those people, such as Broqua or Marc Bertrand?'

She watched them all exchange furtive glances and suddenly realised the answer to her question. 'So, I suppose they'll all have some sort of fatal accident!'

Major Malraux looked at her and answered. 'The waters around here are very dangerous and these people will insist on sailing their yachts out in the Atlantic!'

Carla shook her head as Scott added sarcastically: 'Yes, it will be such a loss to Provençal society, but these boating disasters will happen!'

She looked at him, shocked, but was beginning to understand the intricacies surrounding Scott's world of international espionage.

'Anyway, we must get you over to Frejus and then you'll need some sleep,' said Major Malraux. 'I'll arrange for you to be transported to the hospital first thing in the morning.'

Carla snapped back to her immediate priority. 'I want to go now!'

Pierre intervened. 'Major Malraux's right, Carla. It's too late to go to the hospital and you can both stay with my family tonight – after you've been decontaminated, of course!'

Sensing defeat she turned to Scott. 'What do you think we should do?'

'I want to see him badly as you do, but it is the early hours of the morning and it wouldn't be fair to impose ourselves on the hospital now. Especially as they've finally managed to get him off to sleep. And in my experience, that's no easy feat!'

Carla knew he was right and reluctantly agreed.

Scott grinned and suggested: 'Perhaps we should take some temazepam; that's what they usually administer to soldiers coming off active duty!'

'No, I don't think so. Tranquilizers and ionizing radiation are not a very good combination!'

'On this occasion, Carla, I totally agree with you.'

As they were walking towards the helicopter, which was waiting to airlift them to Frejus, she said to Scott: 'I wonder if they've told Ben where we really are?'

They both laughed.

Ben was lying in bed, very bored, when Carla and Scott burst in early the next morning. His face lit up when he saw his wife and brother.

'Where the bloody hell have you two been and, Carla, have you got my mobile phone?'

Carla looked at Scott and they both laughed. 'I'm sorry Ben, but I've lost it.'

'You've lost it!'

'Yes, sorry. But don't worry; I'll buy you another one and you can use mine for now.'

She ran to him and they grabbed hold of each other.

'Ben, thank God you're alright! You've no idea how worried we've been.'

'How did you manage to lose my phone?'

'It's a very long story. When you're fully recovered, Scott and I will tell you all about it.'

Ben lay back down.

'I don't remember anything that happened, Carla. How did I get shot in the shoulder?'

'Don't worry about that. We'll fill you in with everything when you're better. You need to rest and build up your strength.'

'The doctor told me that I've been unconscious for nearly a week!'

'Is that all, Ben?' she replied pensively. Just for one moment her eyes glazed over. She quickly snapped out of it and added, 'It seems much longer!'

Scott went over to his brother and smiled.

'Welcome back, mate.'

Carla watched as the two brothers hugged each other. *You two aren't the hard guys you make out to be,* she thought affectionately.

After they had released each other, Ben said: 'The doctor also told me that there was a nasty accident last night in the Atlantic. A luxury yacht sank and everyone on board was drowned, including the pathologist from this hospital. Everybody here is really upset about it, because apparently he was a really nice guy. His body's still missing, along with a retired magistrate. The coastguard think they might have been eaten by sharks! Isn't that terrible?'

Scott and Carla exchanged glances.

'Yes, I heard about it on the radio this morning,' said Scott, indifferently. 'Very tragic. Would you like some more coffee, Ben?'

Printed in the United Kingdom
by Lightning Source UK Ltd.
115762UKS00001B/73-75